The Cats of Charnwood Forest

Book 1
By Constantine

Copyright © 2024 by Constantine.

All rights reserved. This book or any portion thereof may not be reproduced or used in any manner whatsoever without the express written permission of the publisher, except for the use of brief quotations in a book review.

Published in the United Kingdom by

Coalville C.A.N. Community Publishing
Memorial Square,
Coalville,
Leicestershire,
England,
LE67 3TU

First Published in 2020

ISBN 978-1-9168960-6-2

Second Edition

10 9 8 7 6 5 4 3 2 1

https://coalvilleccp.uk

Foreword

By Andrew Brenner

The Cats of Charnwood is a tale of two kittens. It begins as Scruff and Bailey are separated from their mother and taken from city to country by their new owner. But life in the country proves more surprising than anticipated. Under the tutelage of Shadow, an older cat, the kittens learn the magical skill of Dream-Walking, encounter mythic creatures and travel through interlinked worlds on their adventures. Elves, Fairies, Goblins, Boggarts and Brownies all play their part as Scruff and Bailey prove to be two of the most heroic kittens you will ever know. As Cats of Charnwood, they are expected to become Guardians, maintaining peace, overcoming their fears, and restoring balance to warring worlds.

I first met the author, Constantine, when he was introduced as a potential writer for the BBC pre-school TV series, Pablo. This show follows the adventures of Pablo who, as an autistic child, sees the world differently. Using his magic crayons Pablo creates the 'book animals', who, as friends and inner companions, help him understand and interpret his experiences. Working together they find solutions to Pablo's problems.

Constantine seemed almost suspicious of both me and this writing opportunity at first, but as he learned more about the project, and as we got to know each other, his confidence grew. In a short space of time, he came up with a series of very funny and original stories. Constantine worked hard, once sending me three drafts of a story at the same time, each one an improvement on the earlier one. His stories were warm, compassionate, and infused with an appreciation for the value of friendship.

The Cats of Charnwood highlights these same qualities in his writing. This tale of fantasy and adventure is a fresh exploration of the folkloric traditions of these islands and beyond, Scruff and Bailey are compelling and lovable heroes. By the end of their story, you like me, will probably be left feeling that there are a lot of things we don't wonder about enough, that might well be worth paying attention to.

Andrew Brenner

November 2020

Ghaz'on

Picture of Ghaz'on, courtesy of Tiya Constantine

For Tiya:

You are always in my thoughts.

With thanks to:
My son Jake for his tremendous help.

My wife Kirstien for endless love and support.

And to Andrew for the endless encouragement and kind words, just when they were needed.

And for all you wonderful readers, there is now a map at the back.

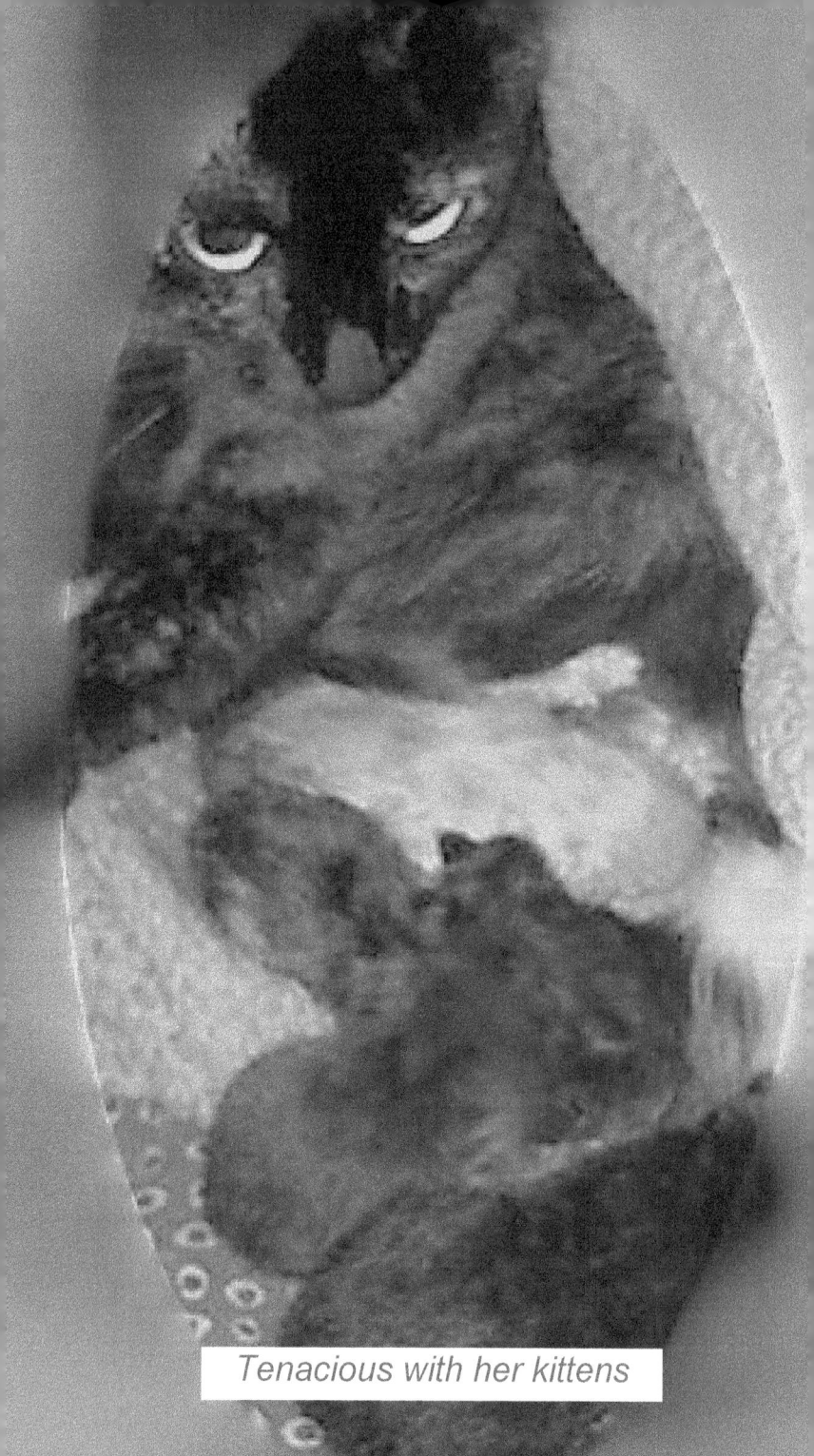
Tenacious with her kittens

Chapter 1
Bailey & Scruff Go North

In a flat in London, there was a bedroom. In this bedroom was a wardrobe and inside, wrapped in blankets, lay a cat, licking her six newborn kittens. The cat's name was Tenacious, and her human was called Jon.

Although Tenacious knew that Jon loved her dearly and loved the kittens too, a flat in London is too small a place to keep seven cats. Jon searched far and wide to find good Humans for the kittens to own. (Humans like to think that their cats belong to them, but any cat will tell you, they own their Humans.)

The first kittens to leave were Whisky (a handsome ginger boy kitten) and Trixie (a lovely grey girl kitten). They went to an old friend of Jon's who lived in Surrey.

The next was Marv (a boisterous black kitten, the biggest of the litter) who was to become the friend of a local businessman.

After that went Jemima, (a beautiful black, white, ginger, and brown kitten). She went to a young lady who loved to look after animals.

The last were Bailey and Scruff. These two went the furthest and on the strangest journey.

***

The journey started simply enough, with a knock at the door.

The kittens had been without their other brothers and sisters for about a week. They didn't miss them much. Kittens are just like that. All kittens know that when they are about twelve weeks old, they move to new homes. So they don't worry about it much at all.

Bailey and Scruff were enjoying the extra time with their mum, who would chase them around the front room and teach them games like 'hide & seek', or how to pounce.

One day a young woman came to visit. She had a cat carrier with her, and Scruff knew what this meant. It was time for another of them to leave. As soon as the young woman sat down, Scruff gave her a sniff and decided she liked her. She smelt different to anyone Scruff had ever met.

A moment later, Scruff climbed inside the box and settled down. She was quite surprised when a few minutes later she was woken by Bailey.

As soon as the door of the cat carrier was closed, Bailey started to cry. The Humans outside made calming 'shushing' noises, but it didn't help. The Humans couldn't speak fluent cat, of course. Scruff opened one eye and yawned.

"Oi, what's all the noise," she said, wiping the sleep from her eye with a paw.

"This box is too small, and I don't know where I'm going, and I don't know what to do, and I want my mum," Bailey replied.

At that moment, Tenacious came over, sniffed the box, took a last long look at them through the bars, and walked away. Cats are good mums and Tenacious would miss her children, but this is just the way cats do it.

Then the young lady picked up the box and took the two kittens for their first trip into the big wide world.

For poor Bailey, the journey seemed to last forever. First, the young lady carried them down a long road. Bailey ran from one end of the box to the other, crying and trying to see through the bars, this made the box wobble back and forth.

"Can you please settle down?" asked Scruff.

"I'm too worried," said Bailey.

After some time, the young lady put the box down. Bailey was just starting to relax when something huge and red and noisy appeared. Its mouth opened with a hiss, and to Bailey's dismay, the young lady picked up the box and carried it on board.[1] Bailey started to cry again.

"Will you please settle down?" said Scruff.

"I'm too scared!" said Bailey.

A while later, the young lady took them out of the smelly red metal monster. They were now in a vast,

---

[1] It was a big red bus. But you probably knew that.

echoey space filled with hundreds of people. Bailey started to cry again.

"Will you please settle down?" said Scruff.

"It's too noisy," said Bailey.

Then the young lady took the box through another door and into an altogether quieter and calmer space. She placed the carrier on a table by a huge window through which the kittens could see people rushing around outside.

The scene outside the window started to move, slowly at first and then faster and faster. Soon the city was flashing by.

Bailey watched through the bars as the houses thinned out and the whole world seemed to turn green. The train gently rocked as it sped its way northward and the clickety-clack of the tracks was soft and soothing. Finally, Bailey stopped his crying and settled down.

***

When Bailey opened his eyes again, he was alone in the box, and the door was wide open. New smells filled his nostrils, not unpleasant, but unknown. Bailey cried quietly.

"Scruff?" Bailey called. "Scruff? Are you there?"

There was no answer, and it took a while for little Bailey to steady his nerves. Softly and stealthily, Bailey crept out of the box.

He could see he was in a comfortable looking living-room. He wasn't quite sure what to do next and was thinking of going back into the box when suddenly, something pinned him to the floor.

"Ha-ha gotcha," said Scruff.

As soon as she had heard Bailey cry out, Scruff had snuck up behind the box and waited for her chance to pounce. Kittens and cats of all ages love pouncing games. As she leapt away, Bailey forgot everything and chased after her. Round and round they ran until Bailey had her cornered.

"You win!" cried Scruff, as Bailey started to lick her forehead. "This place is brilliant. It's our new home. Let me show you around."

She showed him the water bowl and where to find his dinner.

She showed him the litter tray, and as he was a neat and clean kitten, he used it straight away.

She showed him the hallway and the gap behind the sofa where they could hide. She showed him the Human, who was dozing on the sofa. It was Kirsty, the young woman who had brought them all this way. Then Scruff showed him the windowsill. Outside was a lovely little garden, and though the sun was starting to set, they could make out lots to explore.

A narrow path ran down to a small flower bed, in the midst of which was a pond. A little spray of water leapt into the air from the middle of it. Beyond this pond was a hedge. The hedge was very thick, and underneath was very dark, pitch dark. From the darkness under the hedge, two glowing yellow eyes watched them thoughtfully.

Bailey and scruff check out the garden.

***

The weeks sped by, and the kittens grew and grew. They found they loved their new Human very much.

Kirsty renamed Scruff 'Willow', though Scruff preferred her old name. She was quite proud of it. No matter how much she licked herself and no matter how much Kirsty combed her hair, it stuck out in lumps. Some of her hair was longer than the rest, some shorter, and it was immensely scruffy behind her ears.

Bailey grew into a very sleek and handsome kitten, but of the two he was the scaredy-cat. If there were an unexpected bang or crash, he would run to Kirsty's lap, unless she was out, then he would hide under the wardrobe.

Bit by bit, as they grew, Kirsty would let them come with her when she was putting out the washing or doing some gardening. At first, Bailey would hang around the door and cry. Scruff was into everything, smelling out the flowerbeds, chasing the flies and crickets and drinking from any handy puddles. However, Kirsty wouldn't let her go under the hedge; on the other side was a graveyard and she didn't like the idea of having to search it for a missing kitten.

***

One fine September afternoon while the sun was still shining in a hazy remembrance of summer, the kittens had their first trip outside alone. Well, they weren't *really* alone. Kirsty sat in a chair with the sun on her face. She had intended to pretend to sleep, so she could see how the little kittens behaved, but the scent of the fresh-cut grass and the pleasant warmth got to work on her. Before long, she was snoozing happily.

The kittens played and chased each other, not to mention the local bugs and the occasional leaf. However, from above them, on a shed roof a few gardens away, a large black cat watched intently. Its muscles were tense as if it were ready to pounce. Its ears swivelled as if it were trying to catch every sound. Its tail swished this way and that, but its pale-yellow eyes never left the kittens.

After a while, Scruff started to explore closer to the hedge. She knew precisely what she was doing. She pretended to be playing but was purposefully heading towards the exciting unknown darkness.

She was almost there and was starting to sniff under the first branches. Cautiously, Bailey had begun to follow a few steps behind.

Suddenly from under the hedge, two bright yellow eyes appeared and sharp yellow-white teeth which glittered in a stray sunbeam.

"Go back..." the creature hissed. "This is not for you... Not yet."

Bailey cried out, and the two kittens ran to Kirsty who woke with a start as they leapt onto her lap. She looked them over carefully and carried them back indoors.

On the shed roof, the black cat stretched and closed its eyes, it smiled contentedly, and as it did, its teeth sparkled in a stray sunbeam.

The creature under the hedge

***

For the next few weeks Kirsty continued to take the kittens with her whenever she went into the garden, Bailey took a while to get over the scare and refused to leave her side. Scruff, however, was soon back to exploring everything. Well, almost everything, she now stayed a safe distance from the hedge.

A week later they had a visit to the vet which they didn't enjoy at all, though they couldn't remember much about it.

Kittens always need to visit a vet before they are allowed out on their own, but that doesn't mean they have to like it.

A few weeks later, Kirsty picked them up after breakfast and gave them both new collars. They hadn't worn collars before, and at first, they didn't like it much at all. They spent a good hour running around trying to get them off and the rest of the morning sulking in a corner.

That same afternoon a man came round and did a lot of noisy work in the hallway.

Kirsty played with the kittens and told them they were going to get a special surprise. When the man had gone, Bailey and Scruff ventured into the hallway. It smelt different, but they couldn't tell just how. Something to do with the front door, they were sure. But nothing immediately came to mind.

After a few minutes, Kirsty went down the corridor with a big load of washing to take outside. Scruff got all excited.

'*Maybe the surprise is outside,*' she thought, and she jumped up at Kirsty's legs with excitement.

To her disappointment, Kirsty went out the front door and closed it behind her without taking the kittens. Scruff cried out, (which is something she did very rarely) and jumped up at the front door. She could hear Kirsty calling her from outside and this just excited her more. She started running backwards and forwards jumping up at the door.

Click.

Scruff stopped and looked around. At the same moment, she had heard the noise; she had felt the gentlest of tugs at her collar.

"Did you make that noise?" she asked Bailey.

"What noise?" said Bailey.

"Oh, never mind," she said and turned her head back towards the door.

Click.

Her ears swivelled round. It had come from the door. There was something different about it. She backed up a bit, but nothing. Then she took a few steps forward and when her nose was almost touching the door.

Click.

Scruff felt the gentle tug at her collar and put her paw up to try and grab whatever it was pulling her and making all this noise. As her paw touched a part of the door, a small section moved outwards.

She jumped back, stunned at the sudden view of the outdoors. Slowly she backed away, unsure what to do. Outside Kirsty was calling her. Scruff pushed the door again, but again she backed away. Just then from outside came the familiar rattle of the cat treat bag.

Before Scruff could decide what to do, Bailey had pushed his way past her and through the cat flap. Scuff could hear the treats pouring out and Kirsty praising Bailey. She could hear him crunching on the tasty morsels and hear Kirsty calling her. She took a deep breath and leapt out.

Of course, the kittens were too young to understand about the magnets in their collars, which unlocked the new cat flap and made sure only they could get in and out.

***

The kittens loved their new freedom, though at first, they only went out when Kirsty did and came in shortly after she returned. Bit by bit, they spent more time outside and started venturing further away, but never towards the hedge. Every moment they spent outside, however, even when Kirsty wasn't there, they were being watched.

The one thing the kittens didn't do was go out at night. At night, they would run and play in the front room or cuddle up while Kirsty watched TV and had her dinner. Then, when Kirsty went to bed, they would follow, Bailey curling up around her head and Scruff by her feet.

***

One night, however, the kittens couldn't settle, it was very late, and something wasn't quite right. The kittens sat upright. Their ears pointed as they strained to catch something on the very edge of their hearing.

Kirsty turned over in her sleep, snoring gently. As quietly as they could, the pair headed towards the bedroom door.

The noise was louder here, though not by much; it was a strange sound, enchanting, but as cat-like as anything they had ever heard. Out in the hallway, they soon found it was loudest by the front door. They both stood by the cat flap listening intently and after a while, looked at each other.

You know how at times you can look at someone and know what that person is thinking as clearly as if they had said it themselves. Well, with cats it's even more so, especially when they are as close as Bailey and Scruff.

'*We could hear better outside,*' thought Scruff.

'*It's very dark,*' thought Bailey.

'*Well, if we don't go far, we will have the light coming through the cat flap,*' thought Scruff.

'*Ok,*' thought Bailey, '*Let's go.*' And making as little noise as two young kittens could, the pair slunk out of the cat flap.

Once outside, they stopped and listened. The sound seemed to be coming from the back garden. Slowly they made their way to the corner of the building and then suddenly... It stopped.

The kittens froze on the spot, not knowing what to do. They heard a little polite cough behind them, Bailey was too scared to even cry out.

Slowly they turned their heads, and as they did, they saw, silhouetted by the light of the cat flap, a large dark shape with glowing yellow eyes and glittering teeth.

"At last," the shape said. "I was starting to think you were going to miss the first night of school."

Chapter 2
First Lessons

The shape stepped forward. It was bigger than both Bailey and Scruff but undoubtedly a cat. The kittens took a step backwards, but the cat stopped and sat down, silhouetted by the light from the cat flap.

"Now I'm sure you must have many questions, but time is pressing," the cat said. "My Human name is Shadow. You can call me 'Miss Shadow' or just 'Miss', now what are your names?"

"I'm Scruff," said Scruff. "This here is Bailey." Bailey didn't say anything. He was busy looking around for somewhere to run to.

"Excellent," said Shadow. "They are your Human names. What are your cat names?"

Bailey and Scruff looked confused.

"My Human calls me 'Willow' sometimes, but I prefer 'Scruff', 'cos I am," said Scruff, wagging her huge fluffy tail to make the point.

"No," said Shadow. "I mean your cat names. The names your mother gave you."

"Our mother?" said Bailey, pricking up his ears. "She didn't call us anything."

"Her Human and Kirsty named us," added Scruff.

"I see," said Shadow. "Was your mother a city cat?"

"What's a city?" asked Bailey.

"Faraway place," said Shadow. "Lots of buildings, hardly any green."

"I heard Kirsty talking about how it was going to take her all day to get us back from London," said Scruff.

"You're from London?" said Shadow with a sigh. "That explains everything."

Shadow walked up to the kittens. Somehow, they were no longer scared of her and sat still as statues as she gave them a good long sniff.

"Hmm," she said. "Your human names fit you well. We can use them. Now it's time for your first lesson. What it means to be a *Cat!*"

"But I *AM* a cat!" exclaimed Scruff. "I don't understand." Bailey also looked confused. Shadow sighed.

"Cats in the cities have forgotten, or have never been taught, the true meaning of being a cat," Shadow explained. "But out here on the Charnwood, we remember. Cats have abilities that fall beyond the bounds of this world, for we can exist in many. We can move as fast and as silent as a dream and talk with creatures that Humans can't even see."

Bailey's mouth hung open while Scruff looked thoughtful.

"Most importantly, we are guardians of this world, and we have duties," Shadow continued. "To help the poor souls from other realms who find their way here and protect this world from, shall we say, unwanted visitors."

By now, Bailey was starting to get a little nervous and was thinking of running back to the cat flap. Scruff had so many questions in her head that she almost wiggled in anticipation and put her paw up to get Shadow's attention.

"No questions just now," said Shadow. "It's time for your most important lesson, Dream-Walking!" She said this with such authority that both of the kittens sat up and paid attention.

"Right," Shadow said. "On the count of three, I want you both to blink at the same time. Ready? One, two, three."

Bailey and Scruff blinked, and in that tiny fraction of a second, Shadow had disappeared. The two kittens looked around quite startled.

"Up here," Shadow said from atop the roof of a shed a few gardens away.

"Wow! How did you do that?" Asked Bailey, who had forgotten his fear now things had got interesting.

"Both of you blink now," said Shadow, and just like that, she was in front of them again.

"That was 'Dream-Walking'," said Shadow. "When cats are unobserved, we can move at incredible speed. It's difficult to explain but thankfully not hard to teach."

Shadow paused while she looked all around.

"It will be easiest if you are very familiar with the area," she said. "This garden and the side path, for instance, I take it you know them well?"

Bailey and Scruff both nodded and so Shadow continued.

"Bailey, you first. Go to the end of the front garden. When you get there, think about the flowerbed near the pond. Scruff and I will be waiting there. Make the image in your mind as clear as possible. Remember all you know of the path, every stone, and every smell. When you know nobody is watching, leap forward. Remember to keep your mind on your destination."

When Bailey reached the end of the path and had turned around, Shadow and Scruff were just visible by the flowerbed in the back garden.

He looked around, wondering how he would know that nobody could see him.

"You and I will blink on the count of three," Shadow whispered to Scruff.

***

Bailey thought about the end of the path. His total concentration was on it. Like all cats, he had always enjoyed occasionally spending time alone.

To his surprise, the moment Shadow and Scruff closed their eyes, he could feel it. He was overwhelmed by a feeling of exhilarating freedom and the certain knowledge that nobody in the world could see him. He leapt forward, and suddenly the world changed.

Except for the place he was thinking about, everything else became grey like foggy shadows. Fear crept up on the little kitten, and he started to worry about all the things that could go wrong. He lost the image of the flowerbed in his head and at that moment, was swallowed up by the shadows. He was lost.

***

Shadow and Scruff opened their eyes. Bailey was nowhere to be seen.

"Where is he?" asked Scruff.

***

Bailey tried to calm himself, and he did, he recalled what Shadow had said about keeping his mind on his destination. He tried to recall the garden, remembering the smell of the grass and the feel of the dirt under his paws. The image of the pond appeared some way off. He rushed forwards, but as he approached his destination, he felt something holding him back, stopping him from returning to our world.

***

"Stop looking for him, close your eyes," said Shadow to Scruff.

***

Hours seemed to pass for Bailey. He was starting to get scared and wondered if he would ever be able to leave this strange shadowy world.

Suddenly, with a burst of light and colour, the way opened before him. With a cry of joy, he leapt back into our world. Scruff was startled to see Bailey sitting in front of them, but she wasn't going to let her brother see it.

"Well, I could have run here almost as fast," Scruff said. "But I couldn't see you, so I suppose that was pretty cool."

"But I was gone for ages and ages," Bailey said, his brows knotted up in confusion.

"Never, you were gone a few seconds," said Scruff.

"He was not in this world," said Shadow. "When you Dream-Walk, you are in the space between spaces, your own personal realm where time moves like shadows and dreams."

Both of the little kittens tilted their heads and looked utterly baffled.

"Ok Bailey," Shadow said. "Go back the same way, but this time you must keep your mind on where you're going and what you're doing. Don't get distracted. Ok, Scruff, blink... now."

As soon as Shadow said 'now', Bailey could feel the way into Dream-Space. This time it was easier; he passed through and ran towards the end of the path. Then on an impulse, he swerved and ran up behind Scruff. Then slipping quietly out of Dream-space he put his snout up close to her ear.

"Boo!" He whispered.

Scruff was still in the middle of blinking, and she leapt with fright, bristling up her hair and raising her paws. Bailey started laughing, and Scruff pounced on him playfully. This Dream-Walking skill was going to make hide-and-seek so much more fun.

***

Over the next week, Shadow took them out every night. Each time she took them further away from home and taught them different ways of using the 'Dream-Walk.' For instance, they learnt how, by using it, they could jump up onto the tops of fences and walls far higher than they could normally.

Shadow showed them around the gardens that backed onto their own and the little alleyways around these, always leading them, bit by bit, to the northwest.

On the third day, they came to a small babbling brook. Here they stopped.

"This is a brook," said Shadow. "It is smaller than a stream and has natural fresh, clean water in it. It is also very shallow and quite safe. Feel free to try some."

Scruff took no time at all to get her feet and chin and, to be honest, most of the rest of her, quite wet.

"Come on Bailey," she cried. "This water is so tasty."

Eventually, Bailey tried some and agreed it tasted fantastic, but he much preferred a nice, civilised bowl indoors.

For the rest of the night, they patrolled up and down a small section of the brook until they knew it off by heart and had discovered all of the places where they could leap over with ease.

"See how the water flows?" said Shadow. "When you see it from the same side of the brook as your home, it flows from the right to left. Remember that! As long as you are on this side of the stream, you should usually be safe."

Although Shadow had said this last bit in a calming way, it sent shivers down the little kittens' backs.

Each night after this, they would meet at the brook and explore the land beyond. Here the houses started to thin out, and the ground began to rise. Ahead of them was what appeared to be a hill of immense size, and to the right far away but visible in the moonlight was another hill even taller.

"That is what Humans call Bardon Hill!" said Shadow. "Just keep it on your right as you go up and to your left, as you come down, and together with the brook you should never get lost."

"What's the name of the hill in front of us?" asked Bailey.

"Hill?" asked Shadow. "Men call that area 'Warren Hills' these days; long ago it was called 'the High Towers.' However, from Bardon Hill to the southeast, all the way to Thringstone in the northwest, it is all one feature, and it's no more a hill than I am a dog."

On the sixth night out, the kittens found themselves atop the rise Bailey had supposed to be a hill. However, when they reached the summit, they discovered that the land did not slope down again but carried on as far as the eye could see. At the same time, they became aware that they were crossing a border of some sort. It felt like they were walking in the same world they walked every day, and yet were in another world, another time altogether. Shadow gathered them close.

"Did you both feel that, as we came over the rise?" Shadow said. Both of the kittens nodded anxiously.

"That was the Thringstone fault line, created by volcanos on this very spot far, far back in time. Here, what was and what is and what could be, are all mixed together. Many worlds exist here. Keep your eyes open."

The next few minutes were filled with excited questions from Scruff, like 'What is a volcano?' and 'Exactly how long ago is far, far back in time?' and many more. Bailey meanwhile looked around him. He was a very practical kitten really, and while he learnt much from Shadow, there was much he didn't understand and preferred to use his own senses.

Ahead he could see some mounds in the moonlight, with crowns of strange up-thrust rocks, which almost looked like stone teeth. There was a slight electric or metallic smell from there, like the smell of the air after a thunderstorm. But Bailey knew the day had been bright and sunny.

Just to the right, a small wood covered a slope. Tall evergreen trees reached up into the night sky. A strong scent of resin and bark came from that direction. Familiar smells and yet more vibrant than anything he had smelt before.

To the left, the land rose even higher and was covered in short, tough grass. The air that way felt fresh and yet ancient all at once.

Bailey shook his head as dizziness took him and sat down. They were by an old low dry-stone wall, and between two of the stones, many small eyes stared out. Bailey hardly noticed them at first, then one pair blinked, and Bailey gave out a startled mew. Scruff and Shadow stopped talking and looked around. All the little eyes disappeared, but Shadow wasn't fooled.

"You might as well come out now," she said, "and maybe I won't have to tell your parents."

One by one, the little eyes returned, and with a cough from Shadow, they crept out of their hiding places. Whatever Bailey and Scruff expected, it wasn't this.

The creatures were each between three and nine centimetres high. Some looked like old mossy knotted sticks, some looked like dandelion stalks when all of the fluff was blown off. Some looked flat like old leaves in autumn.

"Bailey, Scruff," said Shadow. "I'm pleased to introduce you to the Brownies."

***

The Brownies stared at the kittens. Bailey and Scruff stared at the Brownies.

Not knowing what else to do, Scruff leant forward to give the closest one a sniff. It was one of the wide, brown, leaf-like ones. Just as her nose got close, it wasn't there. Bailey saw it with his own eyes. Or didn't see it if you take my meaning. One moment it was right in front of her nose, and then it was gone.

Bailey looked around and spotted It about half a meter away from Scruff. Now Bailey, as we know, is hardly the bravest of kittens, but this he had to check out.

He crept forward as stealthily as he could and snuck up on the little Brownie, who seemed to be chuckling at the confused look on Scruff's face. Bailey had almost reached it when… it was gone.

But Bailey, as I mentioned, is actually quite an intelligent cat, and he was expecting this. He looked up, and there was the Brownie just a short jump away. Bailey leapt after it, and again it vanished. Before long Bailey was running here and there trying to catch the little thing and each time, he thought he had it, it disappeared.

"How does it do that?" asked Scruff as she and Shadow watched Bailey running backwards and forwards while the other Brownies were almost falling over themselves laughing.

"It is just like our Dream-Walking I think," Shadow replied. "But they can do it whenever they wish, whether they are observed or not."

Scruff watches the Brownies.

"Wow!" said Scruff. "Even when a Human is looking?"

"Humans rarely see the Brownies these days, even when they are looking at them," Shadow explained. "They just see a leaf or a twig or whatever."

There was a long pause. Scruff, thinking that Shadow had finished, was about to ask something else.

"They USED to be able to see them," Shadow continued. "If the Brownies wanted them to, but that was a long time ago. I'm told the Humans used to see them as tiny little people in brown clothes. Of course, Humans always imagine that things they don't understand look just like them.

"Brownies, Goblins, Gnomes, Pixies, they saw them all as little people, and called them all 'Fairy folk.' That, of course, really upset the Fairies."

"What are Fairies?" asked Scruff.

"Trouble," said Shadow. "That's what Fairies are you mark my words."

Interlude

Sorry to interrupt the story, but before we go any further, I just want to mention two things.

Firstly, I should point out to any Humans reading this, that rowan berries can make delicious marmalades and jams, but will give you a very sick stomach if eaten raw.

In point of fact, you should never eat any wild berry, fruit, or nut unless you know exactly what it is and that it is safe. Some can be deadly.

Secondly, I want to tell you about why Scruff had to be told off one day by Shadow.

It was the middle of October, and Scruff had spent the day practising her pouncing. Though to anyone else it probably looked like she was jumping in and out of a pile of leaves.

She was so carried away with her chasing and playing that she chased a mouse and caught it. By the time Shadow saw her, she was holding it proudly in her mouth as she took it home as a prize.

"What are you doing?" shouted Shadow. "Drop that at once."

Scruff did as she was told, and the little mouse just stood there too scared to run. Shadow came and looked over the mouse and, seeing it was unharmed, ordered it to hurry along home.

"Well, Scruff," said Shadow. "What do you have to say for yourself?"

Scruff looked at her feet.

"I don't know," said Scruff. "I saw the mouse and the next thing I was running after it and chasing it and picking it up. I was going to give it to Kirsty. It just seemed like the right thing to do."

Shadow looked at Scruff crossly and then called out to Bailey, who was asleep in the front room and quite grumpy about being woken up.

"Right, you two, there is something you need to understand," said Shadow. She was much calmer now, but still annoyed.

"We are house cats. Our humans give us the best food. There is simply no need for us to go hunting mice or anything else. It is one thing to play with each other, or me, or with Brownies. It is quite another to chase innocent little creatures who just want to be left alone, and that includes birds. Do I make myself clear?" Shadow fixed them both with a stare.

The two small kittens nodded solemnly, and went on their way, though Scruff found it hard to understand. She and Bailey not only played together but being best friends and siblings meant they often 'joked' with each other as well.

Scruff would call Bailey a 'scaredy-cat', and Bailey would call Scruff a 'big fluffy mess.' They didn't call each other names to be nasty, but because they loved each other so much, they thought it was funny.

Scruff hadn't *actually* hurt the mouse, so she didn't understand what the fuss was about. You see, she never stopped to think about how the mouse must have felt.

However, something happened one day, which made Scruff think harder about what she did and what she said.

Right, then.

Did I already mention that it was October?

I did?

And do you know not to eat wild berries?

You do?

Ok, I'll continue.

Chapter 3
A Fairy Dangerous Adventure

The kittens had become fast friends with the Brownies and saw them almost every evening. It was now late October, and the adult Brownies were gathering the last of the rowan berries to see them through until spring.

Often Shadow would leave the kittens to play with the younger Brownies while the adults were hard at work. In this way, the kittens learnt something of the Brownies' language, which was a strange sort of sign language, (Brownies having no mouths, you see.) most of it said with blinks and winks and nodding of the head.

The young Brownies loved to play hide-&-seek almost as much as the kittens did and would run around and play tag for hours. In fact, after a time, the older Brownie children even came as far as the kittens' garden to play with them. Though all Kirsty saw was them chasing leaves or playing with twigs.

Down the lane from where the kittens first met the Brownies is High Tor Farm.

It's the sort of place that has cows, hay and friendly people looking after them. By now, the kittens were old enough to go that far all on their own and they often would. They needed to get to know the forest as well as they could, according to Shadow.

However, today the Brownie children were not by the drystone wall. Scruff went on to ask at the farm while Bailey waited in case the Brownies showed up. The cows were all having their evening hay and were chewing thoughtfully.

"Have you seen the Brownie children?" asked Scruff.

"Hmmm, not today," said a young heifer. "Looks fairy nasty out."

Scruff should have asked what that meant, but she just thought the friendly cow had intended to say, '*fairly* nasty out.' However, the sky was clear with a light breeze and apart from a slight scent in the air, which she couldn't place, everything seemed perfectly pleasant.

Scruff thought of going back to Bailey; but decided to carry on. Further down the road, a Fox crossed her path. Now foxes and cats don't always get on, especially in the wild forest. The two eyed each other and Scruff tried to make herself look big.

"Ha-ha," laughed the Fox. "Don't you worry about me, I've eaten well, and I'm not daft enough to try it on with a Guardian, even if they're only in training."

The Fox nodded its head, and Scruff nodded in return.

"Oh, have you seen the Brownie children?" asked Scruff.

"Hmm," said the Fox, who was feeling very agreeable this evening. "I can't say I have. I've just had an excellent meal courtesy of our friendly neighbours, the monks and haven't seen any." Then with a quick swish of his tail, he disappeared into the trees.

"I wouldn't stay out too late if I were you," the Fox called out as he ran. "It looks like a fairy horrible evening."

Now Scruff just thought he meant to say, 'a *fairly* horrible evening', but the sky was still clear, and the wind was still mild, so on she went to the Abbey.

In the Charnwood Forest, amongst the craggiest crags and the scraggiest heaths, is Mount St Bernard Abbey. When you first come across it, it opens up like a sudden, unexpected, and most beautiful garden carved out of the very rocks that make up the volcanic landscape, which, in many ways, is precisely what it is.

An Abbey is like a tiny village with a church and a monastery where the monks live, work, and study. Monks are people who live very particular lives. The monks of Mount St Bernard were kindly and not only looked after the Abbey and its magnificent gardens, but they also looked after animals and other people, in their way.

Scruff had never been as far as the Abbey before. She found it so beautiful that she did not wish to leave. She sniffed the flowers and ran over the lawns, but

Mount St Bernard Abbey

soon she remembered the Brownies and got back to the search. Scruff went into the apiary. This is where the monks kept their beehives and collected honey. The bees were asleep, and a gentle buzzing came from their houses. In the monastery's fields, there were still a few rabbits about, but none of them had seen the Brownies.

"We haven't seen the Brownies in these parts since the end of July," said a rather large and important-looking Buck. "Have you checked by the mount? If you do be careful, its fairy quiet out there."

Scruff was starting to notice that none of the animals could say 'fairly', but she could spare no time in thinking about it.

Next to the Abbey, there is a high tor of ancient volcanic rock, almost as tall as the bell tower of the monastery itself. Cut into this rock are stairs that wind around to the top. Climbing these stairs, people may look out over the monastery and much of the forest. This particular tor is called the Calvary, and at Easter time, the monks perform a special kind of play there.

The View from the Calvary Tor.

Scruff climbed the stairs looking for any sign of her little friends, but there was nothing. The full moon was shining down, and she could see for miles. She came down the Calvary on the other side and decided that she had best get back to Bailey. She was so lost in her thoughts; that she almost missed them.

In the trees to the left came a buzzing noise on the edge of hearing. At first, Scruff thought it was the sound of night-time insects. Then she noticed lights moving under a large fir tree. The scent was strong now like a sickly-sweet perfume. Scruff crept forwards, and the buzzing became the sound of many voices. The fragrance seemed to make her head heavy. Scruff looked under the leaves and here, at last, after all her searching, were her little friends.

The Brownies were all huddled together, looking quite scared. All around, lights bobbed and weaved, and words filled the air like the buzzing of a wasp nest.

One of the lights stopped for a moment, and Scruff could make out a tiny but beautiful woman with wings, which were like a butterfly's but glowed with a pale light. The woman's hair shone, reflecting the light like a thousand tiny rainbows, and her gown, all silver-green, went all the way down to her little feet.

'*Ahh,*' thought Scruff. '*They are beautiful.*'

Scruff was so mesmerised that she didn't notice for some time what the Fairy, (and it was a Fairy, as, I am sure, you have guessed) was saying.

"I have never in all my years," said the leader of the Fairies, "seen anything quite as repulsive as you, Brownies." All the other Fairies laughed a cruel laugh.

"How dare you look at us with those disgusting faces," the leader of the Fairy group continued. "I don't know what we shall do with you. This world is ugly enough without YOU LOT making it worse."

Scruff heard this, and it made her very cross. Without thinking, she walked in under the branches as bold as anything.

"What makes you think you can talk to them that way?" Scruff asked, but if Scruff thought being so much bigger than the Fairies would help, she was wrong.

Suddenly all the Fairies started flying around and around Scruff, faster and faster. Their cruel voices filled her ears.

"Urgh, what is it?" said one.

"It's even uglier than the Brownies," said another.

"I bet it's never even heard of a bath. It stinks," said a third.

"Is this going to be the new Guardian?" said another. "But it's scraggy and scruffy and messy and UG-LEE."

Bit by bit, the words began to make Scruff feel very, VERY sad. The smell grew worse like cheap nasty perfume filling up her nose and clogging up her head. She felt so confused and scared that she froze and couldn't do anything. She wished Bailey was there.

***

Bailey felt he had waited for Scruff long enough. In his heart, he knew she needed his help. As I have said before, Bailey is quite a practical kitten, and now he wasn't trying to find the Brownies, just Scruff. He knew she was going past High Tor Farm, so he leapt into Dream-Space and in a heartbeat was standing by the cowshed.

"Have any of you seen Scruff?" asked Bailey.

"She was here earlier," said a cow. "She went off towards the Abbey."

Bailey had never been to the Abbey, but from where he stood, he could just make out the bell tower in the moonlight. He leapt into Dream-Space and tried to keep his mind on the Abbey, but not knowing the way made it harder.

Unfamiliar shapes loomed out of the shadows. He was almost there when he tripped and came tumbling into the real world, hitting something as he did.

As he picked himself up, there was a growl behind him. Whatever he had tripped over was large, brown, and very cross.

"Not another young Guardian," the Fox said. "Give me one good reason why I shouldn't eat you."

Bailey trembled for a moment and then remembered Scruff.

"I, I will give you three good reasons," said Bailey. "For one. You will earn the friendship of a Guardian."

"I don't need the friendship of a Guardian," said the Fox. "But I suppose it could come in useful; carry on."

"Ok err… two. The winter is coming in and our owner gives us food to spare," said Bailey. "If you find yourself in need this winter, we will see to it you do not starve or freeze."

"Hmmm," said the Fox. "That's more like it… and the third?"

"The third is that I can do this." Bailey had noticed that the Fox kept turning his head to get at something on his back. All in an instant Bailey leapt towards the fox, jumping over him, and pushing him to the ground. The Fox looked angry until Bailey started to scratch between its shoulder blades.

"Oh… oh that's so good," said the Fox. "It's been bothering me for weeks." After a few minutes, the Fox got up, bowing his head before Bailey.

"Your terms are accepted Guardian," the Fox said. "In fact, I find myself in your debt." (Bailey had managed to remove a few ticks from the poor fox's fur, and that is not an easy job, believe me.)

"Have you seen my sister?" asked Bailey.

"Aye," said the Fox. "She was heading to the monastery, and I caught her scent near the mount. Come, I will lead you there."

The Fox led Bailey onwards for his nose was the better, and soon they were close to the tree.

"Fairies," said the Fox, "I told her it was looking fairy horrible, and so it is."

They could hear the laughter of the Fairies. One had picked up Scruff by the tail and had flown her high above the ground. Calmly, Bailey walked into the gathering.

"Put my sister down," he said. "NOW!" He tried to sound as much like Shadow as he could. It almost worked, and the Fairy holding Scruff had almost let her go.

"What have we here?" said the Fairy leader. "Another baby Guardian? You're almost as ugly as your sister. What makes you think we are going to do what you say?"

The Fairies were starting to laugh again but stopped when they saw that Bailey was not scared of them. He casually looked at his claws as if the Fairies didn't matter at all.

"You're going to let my sister go, and you're going to let the Brownies go, and you're going to go back to your world before I lose my patience," said Bailey, as he looked up and his eyes locked with their leader.

"Oh, and what are you going to do if we don't?" said their leader. "You're not even a proper Guardian yet, you haven't the right to tell us anything."

"Me?" said Bailey. "I'm not going to do anything."

With one small movement, Bailey lowered a branch revealing the huge sharp pointy teeth of the Fox outside.

"My friend, on the other hand, is ravenous," Bailey continued, "and fancies trying a Fairy or two."

The Fox growled, and the Fairies started to back away.

"You cannot let him hurt us. It's against the code. You have to help us," said the leader of the Fairies.

"Us?" said Bailey, "Scruff and I? But as you said, we are not even full Guardians yet... I would run if I were you."

The Fox barked, and the Fairies ran. Bailey, Scruff, the Fox, and the Brownies chased the Fairies southeast to a small pond. In the middle of it was a tiny island and rising from the isle was a door.[2]

On the other side of the door was the land of Fayre, the Fairies' home. Bailey and the others chased the Fairies to the water's edge, the Fairies wasted no time in getting to their island, but here, they stopped and made rude noises.

"You can't swim!" they cried. "Na-Na-Nana-Na!"

"Actually, I can," said the Fox and he jumped into the water. With that, the Fairies hurried through the door, but as they did so, the last one turned back.

"We won't forget this!" screamed the Fairy. "Mark my words, little Guardians, we will get you for this." Then it ran off, slamming the door shut behind it. As it shut, the door, then the frame, and then the whole island melted away like mist.

"Well, hopefully, that's the last we will see of them," said Bailey.

"I wouldn't count on it," said the Fox as he pulled himself ashore and shook himself dry. "Now if you will excuse me, I must go." He nodded to Bailey and Scruff and then leapt off into the grass.

---

[2] Imagine a door. Whatever door you just imagined is what it looked like. That's just the way cross-world fairy doors work.

"Right," said Bailey to the Brownies. "Let's get you home."

When Bailey and Scruff got home, at last, Shadow was waiting for them by the cat flap.

"Well, you have had an exciting evening," said Shadow.

"We can explain everything," said Scruff. "But can it wait till tomorrow? We are so tired."

"No need to," Shadow replied. "I've had a message from the Fairy ambassador about your disgraceful behaviour."

"I…" Bailey started to say, but Shadow had not finished.

"I've also received a message from the leader of the Brownies about your heroic action in rescuing their children *and* a full report from a Fox of quite acceptable character I know. I just want to tell you; that I am very proud of you both."

With that, Shadow gave them both a little lick on the head and sent them both off to bed.

Needless to say, now she knew what it felt like, Scruff never caught a mouse again.

Chapter 4
One Sluggish Morning

Shadow woke the kittens early. The sun had yet to rise. Mist crept from the little pond at the bottom of the garden, leaking out onto the grass. Shadow stood ridged and straight-backed; if she felt the cold, she didn't show it. She looked about, and making quite sure she was alone, she quickly groomed her face, head, and ears. It was important for her to look her best when teaching the kittens. She extended a claw and rapped it gently on the cat flap.

Inside, Bailey was in the middle of a lovely dream. He dreamt he was lying on his back in the sun, having his head scratched while he was fed beautiful big pieces of fish. Scruff, however, was having a different dream entirely. In her dream, she was chased by the buzzing of angry wings and the chatter of cruel voices, suddenly one ear swivelled, then the other and then she was wide awake.

"Bailey," Scruff whispered. "Wake up."

Bailey just rolled over with his paws in the air and gave a little meow. Scruff couldn't help herself. She jumped onto Bailey with a tiny kitten-sized roar, and the two went rolling onto the floor.

"Whoa… What happened?" Bailey asked as he looked around anxiously.

"There was a knock at the cat flap," said Scruff.

"Who is it?" Bailey asked.

"I don't know," said Scruff. "That's why I woke you."

The two got up and crept to the bedroom door, popping their heads around the corner just as another 'tap tap-tap tap' came from it.

"It's Shadow," said Bailey. "What can she want at this hour?"

The two kittens climbed out and stood in front of their Mentor.

"What's up?" asked Bailey, and then he gave such a yawn that when his mouth was fully open, it looked like his head was going to split in two.

"Good morning is what you meant to say, I think," replied Shadow, looking at Bailey with disapproval.

"Good morning, Miss Shadow," said the kittens as one.

"That's better," said Shadow. "Now we are starting out so very early as there is some business for us to take care of upon the Charnwood. However, I just want to warn you before we go, that the ambassador from Fayre has lodged an appeal with the Guardians to have you expelled. He has given another account of what happened that night on the mount. Now don't worry, I'm sure it will come to nothing, but I thought it best to forewarn you."

Bailey and Scruff looked at each other,

'*I like being a Guardian*,' thought Scruff.

'*I like learning things as a Guardian*,' thought Bailey.

"Stop that you two," said Shadow, "If you've got something to say, say it so we can all hear."

"We were just saying how we like being Guardians," said Scruff. "That is, I love exploring, and Bailey loves learning, and we both get all we want with you. We like playing with the Brownies and… and we don't want it to end."

"Don't worry," Shadow said, as she licked them both on the forehead. "It's just a formality, nothing will happen. I'm sure."

Both of the kittens let out a deep sigh.

"Oh, don't you think you can relax *just* yet my young apprentices. We have work to do and things to learn," said Shadow. "Sniff the air. Tell me what you sense."

The little kittens both sniffed the air at the same time and wrinkled up their little faces. It was almost as if their noses had been stung.

"It's all wet and horrible," said Scruff.

"It's worse than that," said Bailey. "It's sparkly like… like a storm."

"That's right," said Shadow. "It will be much worse on the Charnwood. This is a special night, and I need your help."

One by one the little kittens and Shadow jumped into Dream-Space and were soon on the Abbey Road close to High Tor Farm. As they leapt back into the real world, the kittens instinctively took a deep breath through their noses. They immediately cried out in pain and ran around in circles giving little sneezes and yelping. Shadow had to concentrate very hard not to laugh, as it would make her breathe through her nose too.

"You're going to have to breathe through your mouths," said Shadow. "Now take a few moments to get used to it and then follow me."

The kittens did as they were told. It made their tongues feel strange.

"It tastes like that little round copper thing that fell out of Kirsty's bag," said Scruff.

Shadow took them past High Tor Farm, then past the monastery and still they went on, further than either Bailey or Scruff had ever been before. The kittens were already tired when they reached a crossroad. Here Shadow turned right, and the kittens followed her silently. On their left-hand side, a wall towered over them. On the right-hand side, fields gently descended into an ever-thicker fog.

Shadow took them almost six hundred meters and the kittens wondered if it would ever end. Then she crossed the road and took them to a small rise where they could see for miles. Below them, trees lined the slope and seemed to go down into a sea of boiling fog. Vaper rose up In places, creating plumes of mist which broke the fog canopy and were caught by the breeze, creating strange slow streamers.

The kittens had never seen anything like it before. By now, the sun had risen but the mist was so thick that it looked like a pale orb floating in an endless sea of cloud.

"What's down there?" asked Bailey.

"Under that cloud," said Shadow, "is the Black Brook Reservoir, one of the best and the worst things ever to happen to the Charnwood."

The little kittens looked down on the grey formless mass and wondered what Shadow meant.

A strange cry filled the air and far below them, the fog seemed to rise up in several places. It was as if the mist was a huge blanket and underneath it, massive 'somethings' moved. Bailey swallowed.

"No time for questions," cried Shadow as she leapt forward. "Follow me!"

The kittens ran after her. Under the trees that lined the slope, the mist was thin on the ground, and the going was easy. But Shadow didn't slow her pace. On they ran until they came out of the woods and into a wall of grey. Immediately the fog surrounded them. They could see massive shapes moving in the mist, darker grey shapes within the grey, sparking with electricity. If thunderclouds had come down from the sky to graze like sheep on the meadow, it would only have looked a little bit weirder.

The closest of these creatures came lumbering towards them. At least it moved like it was lumbering, though neither Bailey nor Scruff remembered seeing any legs. As it moved closer, Shadow started meowing. Her meow began low, almost like a growl and her voice went higher and higher until it almost made the kittens cover their ears. When Shadow reached the right tone and volume, the creature turned around and headed back towards where the kittens guessed the centre lay. Around them came other cries like the one Shadow had made, some were closer, some further away.

"What are those things?" asked Bailey.

"We're not sure," said Shadow. "We've never been able to talk to them. We think they are some sort of cloud-slug. They just roam over the meadows eating."

"Eating what?" asked Scruff.

"The fog of course," said Shadow.

The kittens said nothing for a while, watching the giant clouds slowly moving backwards and forwards over the ground and just as Shadow had said, the fog seemed to be pulled into them.

"Wow," said Bailey. "Think how handy that would be when it's too foggy for cars to drive safely."

"No," said Shadow. "We must keep them away from the Human world at all costs."

Just then, two of the creatures came out of the mist and Shadow pushed the kittens forward.

"Now it's your turn!" said Shadow. "Do what I did. Start with a low growl and go higher and higher until the creatures turn away."

Bailey and Scruff both tried hard and eventually got the hang of holding the right note. The right note, unfortunately, seemed to be slightly different for each creature. When they had all disappeared back into the fog, the kittens relaxed.

"Why do we have to keep them away from the Humans?" asked Scruff.

"Years ago, one of them bumped into a pylon," said Shadow, "those big metal things with the cables. They are very dangerous. They carry the Humans' electricity. It's what the Humans use to heat and light their homes. It makes their TVs and mobile phones work and unfortunately, it's the same thing that comes out of storm clouds or worse, the stuff that's inside the cloud slugs."

"So, what happened when it hit a pylon?" asked Bailey.

"It exploded," said Shadow. "The Humans lost their electricity for miles around and the cloud slug… didn't survive."

"I see," said Bailey sadly.

As the morning went on, and the sun rose higher, the mist began to lift, and the kittens could see a vast body of water. The strange creatures moved towards the water's edge. It seemed to Bailey that one by one, they slowly and silently vanished away.

"Have they returned to their own world?" asked Scruff.

"For now," said Shadow. "When the fog is thick and tastes of distant electricity, you must come here as quickly as possible. The area around the reservoir borders on many parishes. Across the way, is Shepshed, and to the east is Charley. On the west lays Thringstone."

"And the other cries we heard," said Bailey excitedly. "They came from other Guardians?"

"Yes, indeed, well done," said Shadow. "There are Guardians from Shepshed. Most of Thringstone comes under our jurisdiction, except for the far edge. That is taken care of by the Guardians of Osgathorpe."

The kittens had never heard of Osgathorpe.

"It had once been quite an important place," said Shadow. "But that was long ago when Vikings had lived in the area. The name meant 'Osgood's Farm.' It is one of the furthest points of the Charnwood, and it is a strange place. If you ask me, its Guardians are even stranger, but good cats nonetheless."

Shadow started walking and the kittens fell into step on either side of her.

"There is only one Guardian from Charley Woods, and he more than makes up for the rest of us all together."

"Earlier when you said 'reservoir,' did you mean… that?" Bailey waved a paw towards the water. "Is that the seaside?"

"I'll explain all later," Shadow said. "It's time for introductions."

Slicing through the reservoir at its easternmost tip, there stood a bridge, and it was towards this that Shadow led the kittens. By now, the fog had lifted, and they could see how lush and green the meadow was. To their right, they could see another cat, who seemed old and thin.

Two others were approaching the bridge from the other side. The bridge itself was made of stone and had three arches under which the waters slowly flowed. Shadow and the kittens reached the bridge at

The old cat

the same moment the old cat did. Shadow nodded to the older cat who did likewise.

"Cutting it fine, aren't you?" the old cat said. "Thought we were going to have to deal with it ourselves."

"I'm sorry," Shadow said. "I thought it was best to bring my students." It was the first time the kittens had heard Shadow apologise to anyone for anything. The old cat looked the kittens up and down and then turned his attention back to Shadow.

"Quite right, quite right," said the old cat. "Now I must be off. The meeting is to be held next week at the Menhir." And with that, he leapt off the bridge. The kittens ran to the edge, but there was no splash and no sign of the old cat at all. Shadow chuckled.

"Bailey," she said. "How does one slip into Dream-Space?"

"Firstly, you must be unobserved," said Bailey.

"But where around here could you be unobserved?" asked Shadow.

"Ahh," said the kittens together, realising that as soon as the old cat had jumped off the bridge, he had slipped into Dream-Space and could be anywhere by now. As they spoke, the other two cats slunk up.

Shadow nodded her head politely to them. They, however, managed to nod their heads but continue into a forward roll each ending on their backs and each looking right into a kitten's face.

Bailey did not know where to run, whereas Scruff didn't know whether to laugh. The two strange cats then spoke in rhyme.

> "So, these are the kittens,
> so clean and well-fed:
> one full of fun,
> and one full of dread.
>
> Here stand two kittens,
> so young but so wise,
> who rescued the Brownies,
> to our surprise.
>
> They chased off the Fairies,
> with the help of a fox,
> all orange and brown,
> with little white socks.
>
> But now there is trouble,
> and we're in the middle.
> Shall they start a war?
> Or answer a riddle?"

With that, the newcomers rolled back to their feet, pulled faces at the kittens, stuck their tongues out at Shadow, licked the kittens' foreheads and gave a mighty 'HAHA!' before jumping over the side of the bridge.

This time there were two very loud splashes. The kittens and Shadow rushed to the edge and looked down. Below them, huge rings spread out in the water. But there was no sign of the cats. While they were looking down, a small cough from behind made them jump. They turned around and there stood the two cats dripping wet.

"I'm Tipsy," said the first.

"I'm Tumble," said the second.

They shook themselves dry, splashing water all over the kittens, then jumped back over the side and were gone before the kittens knew what was going on. Shadow stood calmly cleaning her fur and chuckling.

"Those two have got to be the craziest cats I've ever met," Shadow said. "And it's just as well they are."

"Why so?" asked Scruff, "You don't like it much when I'm silly."

"When you are as capable as them and know half as much, I won't mind at all," said Shadow. "Fear is something we cannot afford to fall prey to on the Charnwood, and at the same time, it is something we need."

There was absolute silence from the kittens. Shadow had expected them to say something, but they sat straighter than ever and were clearly waiting for her to continue.

"Fear is a wonderful thing," said Shadow. "It tells you something has changed, and you need to find out what. Or it tells you that you're in danger, or that your loved ones are in trouble. We *need* fear. Do you understand?"

Bailey nodded enthusiastically. Scruff put her head to one side as she thought for a moment and then nodded slowly.

"But," Shadow continued, "fear can paralyse if you don't know how to deal with it. Some people are like me, I deal with it by being quiet thoughtful and logical. I know when Bailey goes anywhere, he is always looking for places to hide and ways out in case he should need them, which is a very logical thing to do. But when you were in trouble Scruff, he was able to act."

Bailey couldn't help but feel a little proud and puffed up his chest. Scruff's eyes were downcast.

"You Scruff are a different sort," Shadow continued. "More like those two, you will laugh at fear and rush in. The difference is that they are always thinking, their minds never stop. If you stop thinking, fear can make you freeze. *That* is when you're in danger."

"I froze with the Fairies," Scruff said, looking at her feet. "I didn't want to, it was all the noise and the smell, I couldn't think."

"It's not your fault," said Bailey. "I had a Fox to help me."

"You both did admirably," said Shadow. "You just have lots to learn. Scruff, you will learn not to be distracted from your goal and to always keep a little bit of your mind alert and thinking. You, Bailey, bit by bit, will become comfortable with your fear and see it as a friend."

The kittens stood for a while, watching the crisp autumn sun play on the water.

"Why did you say the reservoir was wonderful and yet horrible?" asked Scruff after a time.

"That will take some explaining," said Shadow. "Follow me."

The kittens followed Shadow as she told them about the first dam of 1796. When it was built, a great many trees were killed, and many animals became homeless. What was worse was that it had burst one winter's day and led to the drowning of many sheep and possibly some Guardians.

The flood destroyed the land for many miles around. The reservoir was left for almost 100 years. In time the plants and animals began to come back. That was when Humans built the second dam. It was higher and thicker than the first and destroyed even more of the Charnwood.

"That seems to be the way with Humans," Shadow said after a pause. "They don't seem to be able to create without destroying."

"What happened to that second dam?" said Bailey.

"It's still there, you can just make it out over to the west of us. The meadow we came out onto used to be on a hillside. Now all below it is underwater."

Scruff looked at the still waters and tried to see in her mind everything Shadow had told them. It wasn't easy, and she had to ask Shadow how deep the reservoir was.

"If you dropped the whole of your house in it," Shadow replied. "You wouldn't even see the roof."

"Why would they do it?" asked Bailey. "Why destroy so much?"

"You mustn't judge them too harshly," Shadow replied. "The water Kirsty gives you in your bowls, or that you drink out of your taps, that she uses to keep your food bowls and your home clean, it all comes out of a reservoir. Not just for you but for all the animals and their Humans for many miles around."

"So, is the reservoir a good thing?" asked Scruff.

"I don't think it's quite as simple as that," said Shadow. "And it's especially complicated on the Charnwood."

Shadow stopped. They were back on the verge from which they had first looked down on the reservoir.

"You remember I told you that the Charnwood stands on a crack in the world? Well, that crack runs under the reservoir. The first dam that burst was much smaller than this, and it caused so much damage. Many years ago, an earthquake cracked this dam. Luckily, it held, and the humans repaired it. But it could happen again… and then things would be very, very bad."

The kittens looked down on the water, which seemed dark and brooding beneath them.

"But there is worse to consider," said Shadow after a while. "The crack doesn't just lead to Fayre or Bracken, the Brownies' world. It leads to stranger and darker places, and the key to movement between the worlds is water."

"I don't understand," said Bailey.

"My head hurts," said Scruff.

"Do you remember the Fairies' door?" Shadow continued. "It always appears on a tiny island surrounded by water. The Brownies come through a tunnel under a tree which is always half-drowned inside. The Slugs you saw today are a new creature. They only appeared after the earthquake which damaged the dam, and they only ever appear by the reservoir in the mist. As I'm sure you know, mist is made of water. The balance of the Charnwood is very delicate. Be warned."

The kittens had lots to think about as they travelled home for a late breakfast. But Shadow was glad, at least it stopped them worrying about the hearing.

Chapter 5
The Child

With a cough and a splutter, the child pulled itself towards the shore. Its long grey fingers scrabbled amongst the loose stones for something to hold.

The sides of the pool, which stretched from wall to wall of the quarry's bottom-most pit, were steep and the poor creature had to spend some time edging around until it could haul itself out.

Eventually, it grabbed hold of some short wild grass and then after a few moments kicking water, it was out and panting. Exhausted, the child lay on its back breathing heavily, its small rat-like eyes closed, and its long nostrils flared as it took deep breaths through its long pointy nose.

The air was cold, and steam rose from the child's wet shirt, jacket, and breeches. Its stockings were ripped, and the heel of one of its shoes hung off.

Eventually, when its breathing had slowed, it opened its eyes. It looked up into the sky, with its clouds and moon and billions of stars. The little child's mouth hung open for a moment and then…

It screamed and screamed and screamed.

***

Bailey and Scruff were far away.

Close by the old ruins of Grace Dieu, which lie on the borders of the forest, stands a menhir. How long it has been there, nobody knows for sure. A few thousand years at least. So many legends have grown around it that I could spend the rest of this book telling you about them and that would just be the start. But the Cats of the Charnwood used it for one very simple thing. It was their meeting place. A Menhir is a stone, nothing more, but it was specially placed there by ancient humans for reasons we no longer remember. This particular menhir is only about 3 feet high, which is perfect for the cats. As each one spoke, they would sit by the stone, (or very occasionally upon it,) and say their piece.

Tonight, was Bailey and Scruff's formal hearing. The ambassador from Fayre was first to speak and insisted that Bailey and Scruff should be expelled from the Guardians. He claimed loudly and cruelly that a group of defenceless Fairies were lured into a bush and then attacked by the young Guardians.

Hours had passed since then, however, and things were going quite well. Their friends, the Brownies, had come and explained in their strange language what

The Child

Shadow Speaks at the Menhir

had *really* happened. A commission from the Guardians had visited both the Cows at High Tor Farm and the Rabbits at Mount St Bernard Abbey. All of whom confirmed the kittens' story. Even the sly old Fox himself had given evidence and said that no cat on the forest had ever had better students than Shadow did.

As the truth came out bit by bit, the ambassador from the world of Fayre grew red in the face and almost burst with anger.

Suddenly a distant cry wafted over the hills.

"Sounds like one of your lot!" the ambassador said to Fox with a sneer. The Fox was quiet for a moment, his head on one side.

"That's not the voice of a fox," he said at last. "Or anything that goes on four feet under the stars. Shadow, I think you're needed."

"Indeed," said Shadow turning to the head of the council. "Mr Chairman, this nonsense has gone too far, and there is work to be done. Surely you have heard enough."

The Chairman, it seemed, was the thin, wiry cat they had met on the bridge. According to Shadow, he lived wild deep in the heart of the Charnwood.

"It has indeed gone on for too long," he said. "Bailey and Scruff, I find you to have acted in the best traditions of the Guardians." As he said this, he proudly puffed out his chest. The ambassador got up and started to fly away, his wings glowing a dull red in anger.

"You there! Stop, sir!" shouted the Chairman, "I will want the names of the Fairies involved and your assurance they will be looked after and not allowed to go unescorted in our woods."

The ambassador's anger broke.

"You will have my assurance and the list, but mark my words," he shouted angrily. "Shadow will face our justice for the crimes of her students." In the twinkling of an eye, the ambassador was gone.

As suddenly as it had started, the strange cry stopped, and for a moment, even the night animals were silent. Then one by one, the cats of Charnwood Forest slipped into the deeper darkness and returned to their own parishes. Last to go was the Chairman. He looked over the two kittens, and as he did, his voice echoed in their minds.

"Ah... you remind me of me when I was a young" un,' thought the Chairman.

Bailey and Scruff looked at each other and back at the Chairman, their little mouths hanging open.

"Ha-ha, that surprised you," thought the Chairman.

"I thought that only we could do this," thought Bailey.

"Oh, any cat can do it, and not just cats. But you have to be very close like you and Scruff are, or very old and silly like me," thought the Chairman. *"Shadow is one of the best Guardians I know, but she has never been good at this sort of thing. She's far too sensible."*

As he said this, the Chairman pulled a face, and the kittens giggled.

"Am I missing something?" asked Shadow sternly, which caused the little kittens to roll on the ground in fits of laughter. Shadow looked to the Chairman, who was grinning widely.

"Forgive an old tomcat his jests," said the Chairman, "your students bring out the child in me."

"Aye," said Shadow smiling, "they do at that."

"One last thing before I go," the Chairman said, his voice now severe and business-like. "I've lived in this forest longer than any cat, and I've never heard a cry like that. It is not of this world. Beware."

Then silently, the Chairman slunk into the darkness and disappeared.

***

The child stopped screaming, though it sobbed. As the cold set in, it rubbed its arms with its long grey hands.

'Why didn't I listen to my parent?' it thought. *'I was warned never to fish when the moon was shining out of the pool. Now the world is upside down, and I don't know how to get home.'*

The child started to move around, keeping its head bowed from the terrible sight above. Maybe it thought to find a cave or tunnel or somewhere it could hide from that terrible nothing where the roof should be.

Behind it, a light shone, then another. It could hear the unmistakable sound of heavy boots marching on rock. It looked up, hoping to see maybe one of its own people, someone who could help. However, the creatures coming towards it seemed like giants, giants with bright lights shining from their hands.

One of them stopped, pointed at the child, and shouted. The noises these creatures made were strange sounds such as it had never heard before, much less understood. It ran, heading north. The peculiar creatures chased after it, but on stone, it was faster; on the rock, its feet were at home.

Eventually, the stone came to an end, long green strands clung to its legs, but still, it ran. Then suddenly, it was thrown to the floor by some barrier, almost invisible in the pale moonlight. It reached out and was surprised to feel the familiar feel of wire. It had seen many such fences at home. In a moment, it was over and away. The two hideous monsters chasing it could go no further.

"We better report it," said Michael. "Runaway child, I shouldn't wonder."

"Nah," replied Dave. "It was too small, and you didn't see its face, like a bald grey…"

"A bald grey, what?" said Michael.

"Rat," said Dave. "A bald grey rat boy."

The two security men shone their torches over the foot of the fence one more time. A small round object glinted in the light, and Michael stooped to pick it up.

"Well, whatever it was, it was wearing clothes," said Michael holding up the button.

***

Shadow returned Bailey and Scruff home before heading out to find the source of the strange cry, Bailey was exhausted and went straight to sleep on an armchair. Scruff wanted to go with Shadow.

"You might need help," she said as Shadow turned away. "You're as tired as we are, I can tell."

"No," replied Shadow. "It's too dangerous. If I haven't found anything by midday tomorrow, I'll let you and Bailey look while I rest." In the blink of an eye, Shadow was gone.

Scruff yawned long and hard before going back in and curling up on the bed at Kirsty's feet.

***

Scruff woke up late the next day to the sound of laughter coming from the living room. She hurried through to see what the fuss was. There was Kirsty, sitting on the settee, Bailey was lying on her lap, stretched out and purring as Kirsty combed him.

Quite unexpectedly, however, a man sat in the corner chair. Scruff had been looking forward to curling up on it herself.

Kirsty and the strange man were laughing and chatting away. When the man saw Scruff, he got up and walked over to her. Scruff looked left and right for somewhere to hide, but it was too late. The man picked her up and started scratching behind her ears. Scruff *loves* being scratched behind her ears. The man sat down with her, and Scruff decided maybe he wasn't so bad. In fact, he smelt very, *VERY* familiar.

A while later, when Bailey and Scruff had eaten and were no longer being made a fuss of, they went outside, curious as to how Shadow had managed in her search, but she was nowhere to be found. They tried going to her house, jumping on the windowsill, and looking through the windows; but they could not see her anywhere.

"Maybe she's sleeping," said Scruff. "She was exhausted last night."

"I don't know," said Bailey, "I'm sure she would have got a message to us."

Just then, Shadow's human came into the back garden.

"Hello, you two," said Pippa. "Have you seen Shadow? She's not been home all night." Bailey and Scruff looked at each other.

'*She must be in danger,*' thought Scruff.

'*We'll follow her scent. It shouldn't be too hard. Don't worry, we will find her,*' thought Bailey, and with that, they sped off.

Following Shadow's trail was not easy, often the fresh scent would cross with an older scent, and it would take the kittens some time to decide the right way to go. To make matters worse, as they did not know where they were going, they couldn't Dream-walk, so the going was slow.

The trail led to Bardon Hill, the highest point in all Leicestershire. The kittens had wanted to reach the top for a long time and almost forgot their worry. Shadow's scent led to a high shoulder of the hill. But suddenly, by a wire fence, it mingled with another smell, an earthy, rocky sent. Both scents headed towards the distant tors of 'Tin Meadow' not far from High Tor Farm. The kittens followed the trail down the hill. Here the black brook crossed their path, on the other side, however, though the strange scent continued, all signs of Shadow had disappeared.

The kittens spent an hour walking up and down the stream looking for some sign of Shadow. There was nothing. Scruff stretched out in the bank and chewed some grass thoughtfully.

"What if she went into Dream-Space?" she said.

"Hmm, there would be a trace, something," said Bailey.

"What if she went back the way she came?" said Scruff.

"I'm sure we would have seen her," said Bailey. He stretched out and rolled onto his back, looking up at the clear winter sky.

"What about that other scent?" Scruff said. "What if this creature she was looking for carried her off?"

Bailey was quiet for a moment. Some dark clouds were coming in from the northeast, which he did not like the look of at all.

"That might explain it," he said, getting up and stretching. "Come on, let's follow the other trail."

***

Upon the high tors of the Tin Meadow, the child shivered. The air was cold and moving in ways it didn't understand. On the very top of a peek, some of the smaller tor stones had fallen against each other, making a shallow cave and the child squeezed itself inside. The sky of this strange world, which had terrified it at first, was currently covered with something dark and heavy, which felt almost like a roof. For the moment, the child was looking out the landscape, shivering with the cold, but fascinated by the strange white things, which floated down and began to cover the ground.

Bailey and Scruff meanwhile, had reached the Leicester Road. The snow was coming down thick and fast, and the kittens were quite unused to it.

"It's too dangerous to cross here," said Bailey as he looked up and down the road. "We should walk to the top of that rise so we can see the road clearly."

As they reached the top, the wind was blowing ever harder, and Bailey shivered.

"It's getting too cold," he said. "We should head back and wait for better weather."

"Too cold?" said Scruff, who by now had so much snow stuck to her fur that she was beginning to resemble a snowball.

"It's lovely weather, why it's the first time I can honestly say I've felt nice and cool," Scruff said. To prove the point, she jumped into a pile of snow and wiggled around.

"That's because you're a big fluffy mess," laughed Bailey. "But seriously I don't think I can go on."

"Go home then," Scruff said. "I'll carry on for a bit longer, and if I get into trouble, I'll come straight home."

"OK," said Bailey. "But first, I'll see you safely over this road."

"Oh, don't be a big baby," said Scruff.

Just at that moment, a large van flew past. Scruff was only a few centimetres from having her tail squished. The two kittens leapt for cover, and it was some moments before she peered back at the road. They could see now that the border between the pavement and the tarmac had been invisible under the blanket of snow. They were lucky things had not been worse.

"You need to be extra careful in the snow," said Bailey.

"Me?" said Scruff. "You were caught out as well."

"Well… yes. Me too," said Bailey. "But I am off home in a minute, and I'm Dream-Walking it, you're the one stuck out here."

Bailey led the way to the best crossing point. Here he could see up and down the road for a long way. He and Scruff looked right, then looked left, and then looked right again. Happy there was no traffic coming, they walked calmly across. (Many cats who do not know better run across roads, but this is very dangerous, especially when it has been snowing. If you are smart, you will walk at a steady pace. Not so slow that you're being silly, but not so fast that you may slip and fall. You should also keep looking left and right all the way across.)

Once safely across, Bailey gave Scruff a small lick on the forehead and in the blink of an eye, he was gone. Scruff spent no time at all in finding the scent again. It was more vibrant than ever and seemed to head through a field straight towards Tors of the Warren Hills.

***

No sooner had Scruff opened her eyes than Bailey was back in their garden. He came out of Dream-Space close to the cat flap. He had thought of going next door to see if Shadow was home, but he could hear Pippa calling sadly for her missing pet.

Feeling quite sad himself, not to mention tired, Bailey went back inside. Kirsty was still talking and laughing with the strange man. The man's scent bothered him, it was so familiar, yet he couldn't work out where he had smelt[3] it before. Bailey decided to slink into the bedroom and was just about to fall asleep when he heard Kirsty coming up the corridor.

"Aww one of them has come back," Kirsty said. "Jon... come and see."

As Bailey fell into a deep sleep, he dreamt of being tiny again with lots of other kittens running around.

***

Back on the Tin Meadow, Scruff was getting closer to her quarry. She was in the Warren Hills Nature Park. Here peaks thrust up from the ground, which you will

---

[3] I have discovered that some humans in other parts of the world speak English rather differently to the way its spoken in England. So for those people Smelt is the same as Smelled.

remember is already hundreds of meters above the land all around. From the top of the peaks, rocks stick up, almost as if tremendous forces have pushed them up through the ground. Scruff remembered hearing Kirsty talking to someone about the tors and peaks and how they had come to be.

Six hundred million years ago, the part of England we call 'The Charnwood Forest', was a string of volcanic islands. As lava poured into the sea, it cooled and became a special kind of very *very hard* rock. The lava kept pouring out until it cooled into mountains.

Then, eventually, as all things must, the volcanos died. The ash in the air covered the land. It was so thick that with the help of the rain, it became a new kind of rock. This new layer of rock covered the harder volcanic stone and eventually, over everything, grass, trees, and plants grew. Then, over millions of millions of years, the islands all joined up. Later, the rain and the wind worked on the top of the tallest peaks, and eventually, the old volcanic rocks started to peep out of the ground. They are still there now, just you go and see.

Scruff, of course, had no idea how long six hundred million years was. (She was not even sure how long one year was.) She knew she was nine months old, and soon she would have her first birthday. It was now the end of January, and up until now, the winter had been mild.

At the back of the park, near a fence which separated the reserve from 'High Tor Farm,' Scruff reached the end of her trail. A tor of huge stones had made a sort of cave. Out from the cave came this strangest of smells. Scruff thought of heading home. Whatever was in there, she did not want to tackle it alone. However, there was no sign of Shadow and, as the sun was setting somewhere behind the clouds, the temperature began to drop even lower. Scruff doubted if she could manage a night alone out here. She took a deep breath and headed towards the mouth of the cave.

***

The child was starting to fall asleep. It had almost stopped shivering and its eyes were flickering. Now you should never fall asleep when it's freezing cold however much you want to; it can make you deathly ill. The child did not know this, as it had never in its life been anywhere cold. It hadn't even been aware that there was such a thing as cold before now. Suddenly it caught a new scent. It pressed itself against the back of the cave in fear.

***

Scruff looked into the cave. She could make out a slight sparkle of light, and that smell was everywhere. A growl echoed from deep inside.

"Go away," a voice hissed, "leave me alone."

Scruff was very surprised a moment later when she realised that whatever was in there, it spoke almost perfectly fluent cat.

Scruff sat down outside the cave mouth, right in the middle, but kept her head bowed to show she was not a threat.

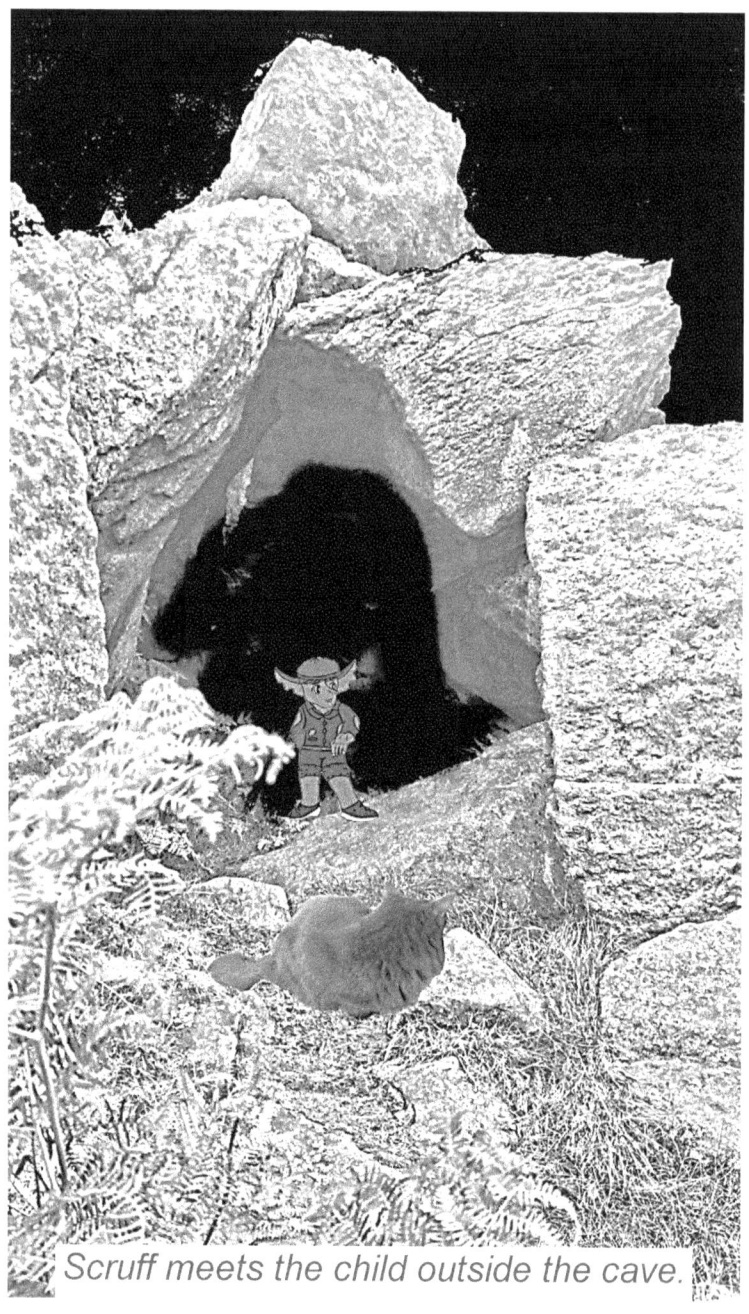
Scruff meets the child outside the cave.

"My name's Scruff," she said. "I am a Guardian of the Forest... Well, I am learning to be a Guardian. Whatever is wrong, it's my job to help you."

"Really?" asked the voice within the cave, and the creature staggered forward into the failing light.

It was short, no bigger than a human who was just old enough to walk. It had very long fingers and a very long nose, and long pointy ears and its two front teeth stuck over its bottom lip. Its skin was grey, and it was wearing human-like clothes that were once very smart and fine but were now ripped and wet and muddy.

"Do you think you can help me find my parent?" it said, and with that, it collapsed.

Scruff rushed over to the poor creature and nuzzled up to it. It was cold. She wondered if she could drag it back into the cave and keep it warm.

Just then, she was startled by human voices. Beams of light showed up the distant peaks and one man's voice in particular was louder than all the other's and sounded crackly like the voices on Kirsty's T.V.

"OK LADIES AND GENTLEMEN," the voice rang out. *"A CHILD WAS SIGHTED THIS MORNING BY SECURITY GUARDS AT THE QUARRY. THE DESCRIPTION IS VAGUE, ANYTHING FROM A TODDLER UPWARDS... OR POSSIBLY A GIANT RAT."* The man sighed, took a deep breath, and continued. *"IT MIGHT BE NOTHING, BUT WE HAVE TO SEARCH EVERY INCH JUST IN CASE. GOOD LUCK."*

The beams of light started sweeping backwards and forwards and were heading in Scruff's direction.

'What shall I do? What shall I do?' Scruff thought, *'If only I could carry it back home through Dream-Space the way my collar comes with me.'*

Then an ingenious idea came to her. She wiggled and squeezed herself under the creature until its arms were loose around her neck, then she concentrated on home and heaved herself into Dream-Space.

The transition was smooth enough, but once in the strange murkiness of Dream-Space, the creature seemed to weigh her down terribly. Her concentration started to waver, and she began to panic. Around her, the shadows loomed and shrunk.

She struggled onwards, worrying about the poor creature, worrying about Kirsty seeing it, worrying about Shadow, and the more she worried, the harder it became until she thought she would be lost in Dream-Space forever.

Chapter 6
Ghaz'on

Scruff began to wonder if the little creature was really all that heavy, or whether it was her worries that were weighing her down. As she thought this, the burden seemed to get lighter.

Her progress was slow, but she was moving at last. She wondered what to do with the creature when they got home. The image of Kirsty's shed came to her mind. Kirsty had recently put an old armchair in there and a quilt, as she had gotten new ones.

'If I can Dream-Walk right into the shed we will be fine,' she thought.

She concentrated on what the inside of the shed looked like until she could see it quite clearly in her mind's eye; she started pushing herself, harder and harder, and then suddenly, with a pop, they were back in the real world. Scruff had got them into the shed.

With the last of her energy, Scruff heaved the creature onto the armchair. It was not as cold here as on the peaks, and she wanted nothing more than to go back indoors and curl up on the bed. But she was worried about this creature. It was cold, and its breathing did not sound right. She curled right up against it, lending it her heat. A little later when she had the strength, she found the plastic bag in which the old duvet was stored and pulled enough out to cover herself and her guest. Then she fell into a long deep sleep.

She did not hear Kirsty saying goodbye to Jon. Nor did she hear her name called and the rattling of the treat bag.

***

Bailey woke with a start, the pale blues and oranges of early dawn were creeping over the horizon, although to Bailey they were dim and hazy. What woke him was the smell. It seemed to be everywhere. He called out for Scruff, but there was no reply. Kirsty's eyes flickered open.

"It's ok Bailey boy," she half mumbled. "I'll get your breakfast in a minute." And with that, she yawned, rolled over and passed out again.

Bailey wandered around the flat, looking for the source of the smell. He could smell it in the front room, but not as much as in the bedroom, and he could smell it in the hallway more than anywhere.

He went out through the cat flap. Here in the alleyway by the house, the smell was stronger than ever but he was getting used to it now. It was quite a pleasant smell really, rich, and earthy. He called out again for Scruff, and a small cry came from behind the shed door.

"Bailey? Is that you," Scruff asked.

"Yes," said Bailey. "How on earth did you get in there?"

"I Dream-Walked in," said Scruff. "I had no choice."

Bailey was amazed.

"Hang on a minute," he said. "You Dream-Walked through a shut, locked door? How?"

Bailey looking amazed.

"I don't know," replied Scruff. "I had to get the creature somewhere safe and…"

"I think you better tell me everything, but first, has there been any sign of Shadow?" asked Bailey.

"No," said Scruff. "The creature hasn't woken yet; the poor thing is exhausted. Though it's warm now and its breathing sounds better. I'm famished though."

"Kirsty will be making breakfast soon," said Bailey. "Come and get some."

"I'm too tired to Dream-Walk just now," said Scruff.

Bailey darted back into the flat and could hear Kirsty starting to move around. He rushed into the kitchen and managed to open a cupboard with his nose. He knew it was a bit naughty and Kirsty didn't like him going into the cat food cupboard, but this was an emergency.

Inside the cupboard was lots of cat food. There was cat food in tins and cat food in boxes, packets of cat treats and all sorts. Bailey found what he was looking for: cat food in a thin pouch. He picked it up in his teeth and carried it outside, just in time, as Kirsty got up a moment later. He bit the corner of the pouch and managed to open it a little, then slid it under the shed door.

On the other side, Scruff tore at the sachet, but could only get a little of the jelly and fish out which she licked up hungrily. The smell, however, seemed to have a remarkable effect on her guest. The little creature crawled from under the duvet and looked around blinking. It took a few moments to take in its surroundings and then it looked at Scruff.

"So… I didn't dream you then," it said eventually. "Where am I, and is that fish I can smell?"

Scruff was so pleased to hear its voice; that she almost dropped the packet. Instead, she brought it over to the young creature.

"Thake thith," she said. She couldn't quite talk properly with the packet in her mouth, but her new friend understood and took it.

"It's food," Scruff explained. "It comes in these packets, and our human feeds them to us. What's your name?"

"My name's Ghaz'on," it said. "Would you… um, mind if I had a little bit of this food?"

"Help yourself," said Scruff. "I can't seem to get it open. Humans just tear the top off, but it's not so easy for us cats."

Ghaz'on found the corner that Bailey and Scruff had been chewing and, in a moment, had the pouch open. It poured some into its palm and held it out for Scruff.

"I don't normally eat out of people's hands," said Scruff, "but I am starving, thank you."

When they had both eaten, Scruff introduced Ghaz'on to Bailey, (who was still on the other side of the door). She then told them both everything that had happened since Bailey had left her. Bailey listened with interest, especially when Scruff recounted how she had managed to get the little creature back to the shed.

"How did you get Ghaz'on through Dream-Space?" asked Bailey.

"I don't know," said Scruff, "maybe it's because Ghaz'on was asleep."

"But how did you get through a locked door?" asked Bailey.

"I don't know," said Scruff, "I was too busy to think about it."

"And how come it speaks cat?" asked Bailey.

"I don't know," said Scruff, "I haven't had a chance to ask it anything yet." And with that, she ignored the endless stream of questions coming from Bailey and turned her attention to Ghaz'on.

"Ok," said Scruff. "Can you answer some questions for me, so I can try and help you?"

"I'll try," replied Ghaz'on. "What do you want to know?"

"Do you know what sort of person you are?" asked Scruff.

"What do you mean?" Replied Ghaz'on.

"Well, I'm a cat," Scruff explained. "And Kirsty is a Human, and some of our friends are Brownies and a Fox and lots of others. What are you?"

"Oh," said Ghaz'on sadly. "I'm sorry. I don't know."

"Don't worry," said Scruff. "Can you tell me the name of your world?"

Ghaz'on looked thoughtful. "We call it Kapul-Tok," it said.

Scruff sighed. "It's not a world I've heard of, but there are people we can ask."

Ghaz'on sniffled. "Please, do help," it said. "I want to go home."

Scruff stretched out thinking, trying to piece together all the things she had learned over her short life and see if there was some clue. Bailey, meanwhile, was still outside the door listening to everything going on and took the opportunity to ask a question of his own.

"Where's Shadow?" he shouted. Ghaz'on looked over to Scruff.

"Who is Shadow?" it asked.

"Shadow is our teacher," said Scruff. "She was looking for you yesterday but has disappeared. Have you seen her?"

"I haven't seen anyone else like you," said Ghaz'on. "But can I ask something? The words 'her' and 'she' what do they mean?"

Scruff sighed. It was going to be a long morning.

***

"So let me get this straight," said Ghaz'on sometime later. "Some of you are male and like boys' things, and are called boys, or he or him."

"Yes," said Scruff.

"Some of you are female and like girls' things are called girls or she or her," said Ghaz'on.

"That's right," said Scruff.

"And some of you are male and like girls' things but are still called boys and some are female and like boys' things but are still called girls?"

"Well, yes…basically," said Scruff.

"That's silly," said Ghaz'on.

"Well… tell me what it's like in your world," said Scruff.

"Well, in our world, we are all called only by our names," said Ghaz'on. "And, of course, our jobs are important."

"So what do you call your parents?" asked Bailey. "Mum? Dad?"

"We call our parents 'parents' or sometimes, 'rents' for short, and being a parent is a vital job," said Ghaz'on. "My parent looks after about 30 children but still makes time for each of us. There are other jobs: miners and builders, and fishers, and teachers. But being a parent is probably the most important job one can have and is very respectful. Everyone looks up to their parents. Some of us have two or three jobs, but when you're a parent, that's your only job, even if you only have one child to look after, 'cause looking after a child is a full-time job. I think I might like to be a parent one day. But I also like fishing."

"And would you not say one of your parents is a 'mother. or a 'she'?" asked Scruff.

"No, I wouldn't," said Ghaz'on. "In our world, it doesn't matter what job you do, what games you play, what you look like, what clothes you wear. It doesn't matter whether you are average or different, or ill, or whether you are clever or not. We are all 'Kapul,' and that's all that matters."

"What does 'Kapul' mean?" asked Scruff.

"It means us," said Ghaz'on. "It's just what we call ourselves."

"Well…" said Scruff thoughtfully. "Maybe the Chairman will know what it means."

When she was feeling up to it, Scruff went into the flat for a proper breakfast. While she was there, Kirsty made a good deal of fuss over her and subjected her to a thorough grooming. It is essential for scruffy, long-haired cats that their humans give them a good combing at least once a week if not more. Bailey spent some time talking through the shed door, answering Ghaz'on's questions about our world. Ghaz'on was still scared of the terrible nothing above him. Bailey did not understand.

"It's just the sun, up in the sky," he said, "It can't hurt you."

"We don't have a sky in our world," said Ghaz'on. "Suns shine up out of the lakes during the day, and moons shine up out of them at night, and there are many lakes in different caverns. Some have one sun, and some have two or three. Some have no moon, and some have several."

"How do you get from one cavern to another?" asked Bailey.

"Tunnels," said Ghaz'on. "We are brilliant with tunnels. We tunnel and mine and dig. We dig up and down and all over."

"But..." said Bailey after a pause. "If you dig up, you must eventually reach the surface, a place that's like our world!"

Ghaz'on shook his head, his brows furrowed in confusion.

"Why?" it said. "Our world does not have a 'surface' and doesn't need one. We could tunnel up forever and ever and never find any *'surface'*, just more caverns and lakes."

"I can't say I understand," Bailey said, "but maybe that's because we are from such very different worlds. In our world, the sun, and the moon, shine down onto the pools, not up out of them."

***

The evening was coming in when they set out. Scruff had wanted to leave at nightfall, but Bailey had been paying attention to all the parts of Shadow's lessons that Scruff had found boring.

"Evening is when it's best to slip past humans unnoticed," he explained. "During the day, humans see better than us over long distances. So, it's no good to go then. At night, their vision is not as good as ours, but they are on alert and likely to spot things."

Scruff considered this and then nodded her agreement.

"Dawn and dusk," Bailey continued, "when it's not quite light or dark, that is when humans are likely to dismiss something they don't understand as a 'trick of the light.' As the dawn has already passed, this evening will be our best chance."

***

Getting Ghaz'on out of the shed had been difficult. There was just no way to get it through Dream-Space when it was awake. Bailey suggested knocking the poor creature unconscious, but neither Scruff nor Ghaz'on were keen on this plan.

Scruff eventually found the solution. She asked Ghaz'on if it knew any songs, and it knew many. She then got underneath Ghaz'on while it was still under the duvet and got it to sing one of its favourites. It closed its eyes and started singing a deep, slow song all about digging delving, and building. It went something like this:

> "In Kapul-Tok, we dig and play,
> By lakes, which fill with light of day,
> In the water, we catch fish and play,
> When the moon appears, we run away."

The song seemed to make Ghaz'on sad, so sad in fact, that he barely noticed that while he had been singing, Scruff had moved them right through Dream-Space to the other side of the door.

"I wish I had listened to the old song," Ghaz'on sniffed. "Then I wouldn't be in this mess."

"What do you mean?" asked Bailey. "How would the song have helped."

"One of the earliest things they teach us is to stay away from the lakes when the moon shines up out of them," said Ghaz'on. "They were digging a new tunnel and came across a new pool. Our teachers and parents told us to keep away, but I wanted to surprise my parent, Dzukaluke. Dzukaluke loves fish more than anyone I know, and I thought I could catch some as a present. So I snuck out in the night, and I slipped in the dark. The next thing I knew, I was here."

"Hmmm," mused Bailey. "Remember to tell all this when we get where we are going. It might be important."

"Where are we going?" asked Ghaz'on.

"Into the heart of the forest," said Scruff.

The place they were heading to was not *literally* the centre of the forest. If you were to look at it on a map, it would appear only to be one corner of it. But it was the oldest part.

One thousand years ago, the area of Charley Wood was also known as Cernelega, and it was from this that the word 'Charnwood' came about.

Whatever its origins, it was further than the kittens had ever been, and they were not comfortable having to walk there. It was simply not possible to Dream-Walk that far without knocking poor Ghaz'on unconscious, and even then, it might not work as they hadn't been there before.

So they walked, deciding to take the straighter paths along the roadways despite the danger, for they needed speed. They hurried along as fast as they could, flitting from cover to cover.

In no time at all, they had crossed the Black Brook and were heading up to the crossroads. Here they rested in the shade of the very wall where they had first met the Brownies; it seemed an age ago. Then they were off again, heading southeast. Before long, the pavement disappeared, and they had to hide in the long grass and snowbanks as many cars and lorries went by.

Now on that stretch of the road, there is a pub known as The Bulls Head. As the three of them passed, a man leaving the Pub and opening up his car got a good look at Ghaz'on. He looked away, blinked, and looked back again. By then Ghaz'on was gone, so the man did something very sensible. He put his car keys back in his pocket and phoned for a taxi.

About a mile further on, Ghaz'on and the kittens left the main road and took a narrow footpath. The darkness was almost complete, and the kittens were nervous, they were heading into Charley Wood. They had never been here before, and they felt like a million eyes were watching them.

"Where now?" asked Scruff.

"I don't know," said Bailey, "I only know he lives in Charley Wood. But I'm not sure exactly which part of Charley Wood. I haven't got his address."

"I was told he lived in the 'Wildcat Wood," said Scruff, "which is around Cat Hill."

"Which direction is that?" Bailey asked. Scruff looked at her feet.

"I don't know," she said.

"Well, we can't just wander around and hope," Bailey said. He looked around at the trees, which seemed the same in every direction, "Maybe we should just shout?"

'I wouldn't do that if I were you,' said a familiar voice in the kittens minds. *'You are Guardians and should always appear calm and in control.'*

'Where are you?' thought both Bailey and Scruff as one.

A small cough made them turn around and behind them stood the Chairman of the Guardians.

"How did you find us?" asked Scruff, "We don't even know where we are."

"I have many ways of getting news," said the Chairman. "And your thoughts have not been hard to read as you approached Charley Woods. To answer your question, Bailey, this is Burrow Wood. The wood of the wild cats is to the north."

The Chairman walked up to Ghaz'on, circled it, sniffed it, then sat down and scratched behind his ear.

"Well, I think you had better tell me everything," he said.

The moon was rising as they got to the end of the story, and the Chairman was concerned.

"This is most worrying," he said. "Shadow is one of our most trusty Guardians. For her to simply disappear? Why, it's unheard of."

"Look," said Ghaz'on, "I'm sorry you have lost your friend… but any ideas on how to get me home?"

The Chairman looked Ghaz'on up and down and gave it another sniff.

The Narrow Bridge

"I'm sorry," he said. "There are certainly enough clues, I just don't know what you are. Your clothes suggest a level of craft close to human. Your language is almost pure cat-speak. Your scent is earthy. That should be enough clues, but I have no idea."

The Chairman sat and sighed, then an ear popped up and swivelled, then the other.

"Of course," he said. "I may be the oldest Guardian on the Charnwood but there are things older still… follow me, all of you."

He walked off deeper into the forest. The kittens tried to ask him questions, but just received a 'shhhh,' in reply.

"Are we going to your home?" asked Scruff and to this at least she got an answer.

"I don't have a home," said the Chairman. "I have several."

"Several?" said Scruff. "How? Why? What?"

The Chairman chuckled, "Some cats are house cats and never go out," he said. "Some are like you, who have a single home and a dedicated human. Some cats are totally wild and have no homes. Some are like me. I have several homes. The humans in each one think of me as a member of their family and feed me. Each one gives me a different name, but they all know I go to other families when I wish to. It's a good life for me, but it's not to everyone's tastes."

"I don't think I could ever live with anyone but Kirsty," said Bailey.

***

After a time, they reached a small brook, which seemed to be almost dry. The few patches of snow that had made it through the canopy seemed to be all the water it contained. Across the brooks channel, a narrow wooden bridge had been placed.

On the other side, right by the path, a hole led underground. Bailey supposed it must have once been a Burrow or Set. He didn't want to upset a family of sleeping Foxes or Badgers (and neither should you). But other than a small colony of Miner Bees, who were dozing in one of the walls of the tunnel, it was quite deserted. The Chairman led them ever downwards, and the floor and walls became wet and slippery. Then the tunnel opened up into a wide chamber half-filled with water.

Scruff reasoned that they must have been directly under one of the old trees, as roots surrounded them like pillars holding up the hall. Towards the north end of the hall, two roots grew close together. Between them was a hole. At first, Bailey thought it to be the start of another tunnel, but there was no tunnel, just this half-submerged gap into nothing.

"I must leave you for a moment," said the Chairman. "Or several moments. I'm never sure, to be honest." And with that, he jumped into the hole and vanished.

More than a few moments went past. On the Charnwood, the moon was now high, and the night was starting to get old. Outside the woods, the snow was beginning to come down on the peaks, and the temperature was dropping. Though it was warm enough in the chamber.

Bailey, Scruff and Ghaz'on were getting grumpy. Nobody likes standing around in the water, in almost pitch dark with nothing to do. Suddenly Bailey jumped in shock, making a huge splash. From nowhere, floating on the water, a leaf with legs appeared.

"Whithhh?" he said. "Hey, Scruff! It's Whithhh, the Brownie."

From out of the hole, came many more of the kitten's Brownie friends, and behind them came the biggest Brownie the kittens had ever seen. It squeezed out of the hole, looking like a bush, walking around on its roots. It had several arms, which ended in leafy hands and down where you would have expected its tummy to be, there were several shiny bright eyes.

No sooner had this giant of a Brownie come out that the Chairman came splashing up behind them.

"Sorry I was so long," he said. "But the Brownie Elders are mostly asleep this time of year. Took a heck of a time to wake them up." The Chairman introduced the kittens and Ghaz'on to the giant Brownie.

"This," he said, "is WhooWhee, an elder of the Brownies, if anyone can work out how to get young Ghaz'on back home, it's her."

The elder Brownie took a few steps towards Ghaz'on, who was shaking with fear. She looked at him from a few angles and then spoke to the Chairman in that strange waving language, which made her look like a small tree blowing in the wind.

"She's asking what you call your world," said Scruff.

"It's called Kapul-Tok," said Ghaz'on. The Brownie started shaking all over and Ghaz'on almost ran away.

"It's ok," said Bailey. "She was laughing… Now she's saying that she hasn't seen your kind for over a thousand years and never thought she would again."

"Does she know what I am?" asked Ghaz'on. The elder shook some more.

"She says she does," said Bailey. "Apparently you're a Goblin." There was silence for a few moments.

"What's a Goblin?" asked Scruff. "I've never heard of them before."

"Can we please get out of this water first?" asked Bailey.

***

Back above ground, the Chairman took them to an old, abandoned building. Humans were banned from the area as old buildings are very dangerous. Even the Chairman only used a small part of the shed that was mostly intact.

"I'm not surprised you have never heard of Goblins," said the Chairman. "I thought they were just a legend up until now. In all the stories I've ever heard of them, they were nasty creatures, always stealing and hurting people."

"We're not like that at all," Ghaz'on cried. He was quite upset at hearing his kind spoken of like that.

The Brownie elder interrupted and what she had to say was so amazing that it was a little while before the kittens remembered that Ghaz'on couldn't speak

Brownie. However, this is the elder Brownie's story as the kittens told it.

***

"In the deep past, the worlds were united and at peace. Two worlds were renowned above all others. Kapul-Tok was one of them, for the world of Kapul-Tok was the gateway to all other worlds. Within the world of the Goblins, there are many lakes, each one leading to another world. It was through the lakes of Kapul-Tok that Brownies, Goblins, Sprites, Gnomes, and all manner of creatures could share wisdom and trade goods. Even Humans once, it is said.

"Of these worlds, the most beautiful and enlightened was the world of Alfhiem, home to the Elves. Some say that cats themselves originated there and came to earth. Others say it was the other way around. If one thing is certain, it's that Alfhiem was the highest seat of learning. Their people were peaceful and generous and shared their knowledge with everyone.

"For many thousands of years, there was the greatest friendship between Alfhiem and Kapul-Tok, but long ago things changed. Goblins accused the Elves of using their tunnels and lakes without permission, of stealing the goods they bought and sold, and even of attacking their settlements. The Elves started accusing the Goblins of raiding them in the middle of the night.

"Eventually, war broke out. It was a war that was waged for hundreds of years. That was the Great War between the Elves and the Goblins, which even humans, remember in legends and stories.

"The Elves and Goblins both had colonies in other worlds and so the fighting spread. Eventually, the Goblins withdrew into Kapul-Tok. They sealed off all the lakes that lead to populated worlds, thus stopping the war and preventing travel between worlds.

"As the Goblins were shutting themselves off and sending all of the ambassadors home, the Brownies' own troubles began, for we learnt a great secret and have been unable to do anything about it until now.

"Our ambassador to Kapul-Tok was returning home for the last time when he caught a conversation between two creatures in a tunnel.

"'The Queen's plan goes well,' said one voice. 'The Elves are retreating, and soon they and the Goblins will be cut off. Then we will take control.'

"'Are you sure it will work?' said the second. 'If they cover up the lake to our world, how will we travel?'

"'Through the Human world, we can still travel there through the Thringstone Fault. From there we can reach a handful of other worlds, and once we control them, we will turn our attention to Kapul-Tok.' There was a pause, and then the second voice spoke again.

"'But if, as the Queen says, all other worlds are ugly and hideous,' it said, 'why should we want to travel to them? Is it not enough to prevent them from coming to us?'

"'No,' replied the first. 'We must make them like us, and those that won't become like us, we will destroy.'

"'What of the Elves? They are very wise. Will, they not find another way?'

"The first voice laughed a cruel laugh. 'We have them so terrified they will never leave Alfhiem again. No, like all others, they will fall before us.' As the Brownie ambassador shook with rage, they heard her rustle and chased her through the tunnels. She looked back just as she managed to dive into the pool back to Bracken and saw that they were Fairies. Once through, the Goblins sealed the pool. The Fairies have been hounding the Brownies ever since."

***

When the kittens had finished translating the story, there was a long silence. They were all trying to take on board the enormity of the situation.

"I had no idea," said Ghaz'on at last. "We have learned about the wars, of course. But we are told stories of evil bright-eyed Elves in dark armour leaping out of the water and attacking us as we sleep. I have never even heard of the Fairies before."

"This is news to me also," said the Chairman. "I understand why the Brownies have kept quiet all this time. Without evidence, it's just rumour. We must be cautious."

"If the travel between worlds is impossible now, how do you and the Brownies and your friends manage it?" asked Ghaz'on. Both Bailey and Scruff looked to the Chairman. The same question was in their minds.

"I would have expected Bailey and Scruff to have answered this one for you," said the Chairman, as he looked at the kittens with a twinkle in his eye. "The

Charnwood Forest is on the Thringstone Fault, and the fault allows travel to a handful of the old worlds. But the fault does not work like your pools. It is unstable and can lead to stranger and darker places." He paced around in a circle for a few moments before turning to Ghaz'on.

"And you, young Goblin," he said. "When you get home, you must tell people the truth and tell them that the Charnwood Forest stands with them."

"And how do I get home?" asked Ghaz'on.

WhooWhee bowed and bent, and the Chairman chuckled.

"It's quite simple," he said. "When the moon shines on certain pools in our world, it shines out of other pools and lakes in yours."

Ghaz'on nodded, and the Chairman continued.

"At this time, things from your world can come to ours. When it's the SUN that shines on a pool, things from this world can go to yours. This is when you should return."

The Goblin nodded thoughtfully. "How long before the sun comes up?" it asked.

"A few hours more," said Bailey, "I suggest we sleep here a while and then head out."

***

The kittens did not sleep well, but they did manage to sleep, all huddled together for warmth. As the sky started to lighten, they set out. The traffic was already beginning to build up with people heading to work when they reached the road. Now at least they didn't need to walk along the grass verge, for on the other side was Bardon Hill.

Before going any further, the companions took stock. The last thing they needed was for anyone to see a Goblin, or even worse, see it dive into a pool and disappear.

"It's a pity you can't just jump in from the top of the hill," said Bailey "But It must be hundreds of meters."

"At least 300 meters down to the pool at the bottom," said Ghaz'on. "I've dived further."

"You must be kidding," said Scruff. "You've jumped all that way? Into water?" The very thought had her shivering all over.

"Oh, easy," said Ghaz'on. "Some of our lakes and caverns are huge."

They walked to the top of Bardon Hill as the sun climbed out of the mists in the east. As they went, they spoke of this and that like they were old friends. They were laughing and joking when they finally reached the summit.

Ghaz'on looked out at the landscape all around and then turned to the kittens.

"Thank you for everything," said the Goblin child. "I'm going to miss you, and your world. I might even miss this silly old sky of yours."

On the Shoulder of Bardon Hill.

Before they could say anything more, he dived off. A moment later, there was the slightest splash, but by the time the kittens got to the edge and looked down, there was nothing. It was as if Ghaz'on had never been.

***

There was nothing to stop the kitten's Dream-Walking now, but even so, they walked half the way home. They talked about the Goblin and Shadow and what to do next. It was clear that they needed rest before they went looking for Shadow. When they got home, Kirsty was up and overjoyed to see them.

"Where have you two been?" she asked. "I've been worried sick. The lady next door has lost her cat, and I was scared you had gone missing too." Kirsty fussed over them for the rest of the morning, feeding them, combing them, and giving them treats.

"Now I have to go out, I'm off to see Jon. Wish me luck!" she said and hurried out the door.

The kittens were too exhausted to wonder what she meant, and they were soon asleep. They slept long, and it was dark again by the time they got up.

Kirsty was still out, so they fed themselves and went looking for Shadow once more, with no success.

They came home just before dawn. Kirsty was tucked in bed, and the kittens decided to join her. Just as they were falling asleep, they heard something in the garden, and looking through the window, saw two creatures climbing out of Kirsty's little pond. Scruff growled and ran out into the garden, Bailey close behind.

"Who are you? What do you want? Where is Shadow?" Scruff cried.

The two creatures were dressed in armour with swords and shields but were clearly, and to the Kitten's surprise, Goblins.

"Hail!" one of them said. "We have not long before your sun comes up and we can return. We have come to thank you for getting Ghaz'on home, and to give you this."

It handed a small white rod, like a snail shell, to Bailey.

"If you need us," the Goblin said. "Drop the rod in the pond by day, then we will visit one hour before dawn. Ghaz'on has told us about the Fairies, and if the story is true, we will speak more."

With that, the sun came over the horizon, and the two Goblins jumped into the pond and vanished.

Bailey hid the shell near the pond, and they made their way back to the house. It was then that they received their last shock of the day.

On the cat flap, in letters, which only a cat could see or smell, was written:

Shadow is still alive:

Chapter 7
The Search for Shadow

Bailey and Scruff were not happy. Finding the message on the cat-flap had, for a time, given them hope. The kittens, the Fox, the Chairman, the Brownies and all their friends joined in the search. However, as the days turned into weeks and the weeks crept into months, their hope started to dwindle.

The loss of Shadow had affected everyone. Shadow's human, Pippa, had stopped coming out as she was too sad. Kirsty missed talking to her in the garden, and so it made her sad, too. In fact, the whole neighbourhood seemed to have become a gloomier place.

The Chairman himself had come and read the message on the cat-flap. He had sat there for hours pondering and scratching behind his ear.

"If it was written by a friend, then why didn't they give us more information?" The Chairman said, (as much to himself as to the kittens.) "And if it was written by an enemy, why are there no demands, no threats? I'm afraid I don't have any answers. I would think the message is hopeful and we should stay hopeful. But

I'm afraid I can't tell you anything you don't already know, it's most peculiar..."

That was over a month ago.

To make matters worse, Kirsty's friend Jon had been visiting more and more, sometimes staying for days. Then just as the kittens were getting used to him being around the place, he disappeared again. It was very frustrating.

When he arrived, they were grumpy at his smell, the sound of his voice and even his snoring... all of which they found oddly familiar. For some reason when Jon stayed, Bailey kept having dreams about a large black and brown cat, which he was sure was his mum.

Then when he left, they had to get used to being without his noise and smell and snoring and the way he gave them lots of treats and affection. It was very, VERY annoying.

They still had their regular duties to attend to. A few weeks after Shadow disappeared, the weather had turned bitter. Fox had come to ask Bailey to keep up his end of the agreement they had made so long ago. Bailey did so, of course, and Fox was fine.

Then, one day, a party of Gnomes got lost in the snow. Now you might have seen the painted Gnomes that people keep in their gardens, and you may have noticed that they often have strange, bearded people sitting on them with fishing rods. Nobody is quite sure why Humans do that. As anybody who has met a Gnome will tell you, they resemble a toadstool, not a mushroom with a tiny fat man on its head.

However, looking for things which resemble white toadstools in white snow is not an easy job, and that took Bailey and Scruff a lot of time and a lot of energy.

It was now March, and the weather was wet and windy. But once again, the kittens were getting ready to go and search for Shadow.

"Where shall we go tonight?" asked Bailey.

"I don't know," said Scruff. "Where have we not looked a million times already?"

Bailey stared out into the garden, remembering the first time they had encountered Shadow, though they didn't know at the time that it was her.

"Hang on," said Bailey. "The graveyard next door. We have never looked in there."

"Shadow said we shouldn't go in there," said Scruff.

Bailey was quiet for a while, padding backwards and forwards as he thought.

"I'm going to risk it," he said at last. "She could be there, and we would never know 'cos we never looked."

Scruff was not happy. The thought of going in there made her tummy feel all squelchy.

"I think I'd better sit this one out," she said. "I won't be of any use to you in there. It scares me."

Bailey couldn't believe his ears.

"You? Scared? I have never heard you say such a thing," he said. "Well... OK... but if you don't hear from me in an hour or so, do what you can. Bye."

Before Scruff could say anything to stop him, he leapt through the cat-flap and into the darkness.

***

The rain had stopped, and a mist was rising from the ground. You would almost have thought it was Halloween… but it wasn't.

At first, Bailey wasn't sure what all the fuss was about. It was just a big field full of grey stone things. But as the night wore on, he started to get jumpy.

There is something about graveyards at any time and especially at night, which deadens sound. And the silence was beginning to get to him. He started jumping at the slightest thing and had the feeling something was watching him.

He found some of Shadow's scent not far from the back garden, but it was old. Other than that, there was no trace.

He was on the far side of the graveyard when he decided he had searched enough. Clouds were getting heavy, and the mist was cold, so he decided to Dream-Walk home.

***

Scruff was worried. Bailey was late, and everything felt uneasy. The air was charged like anything could happen.

Now I just want to reassure anyone reading this that I'm sure the graveyards near you are lovely safe places. This one, however, is on the Thringstone Fault and as Shadow had told the kittens, the fault does not just lead to Bracken or Fayre, or Shroom (land of the Gnomes). It also leads to stranger and darker places.

***

Something was wrong in Dream-Space. The usual dim grey ground seemed to stick to Bailey's feet. Hundreds of tiny see-through hands reached up like blades of grass and grabbed hold of him. Pulling him down, deep into the ground. He cried out, and with all his strength, he tried to visualise the way home.

Pop!

He opened his eyes, and he was back in his own garden. Only everything about it was wrong. Above him, a black sun shone in a white sky. The grass was black, and the stones were white. The house itself wasn't just black. It almost seemed to be waving in the wind. Its edges were like mist.

He called out for Scruff, but there was no answer. He went to the door, but there was no cat-flap in it. He cried out for help, and something heard him.

From under the bushes, which now had white stems and dark grey leaves, something approached in the shape of a cat.

It looked so much like Shadow at first, that Bailey almost called out. Then he noticed this thing had a long tail, an impossibly long tail. Its ears were odd, one was far too big, and the other seemed way too small. Its eyes were black with white pupils.

"Hello," said Bailey, quite nervously. "Who are you?"

The Other sat with its head on one side and was silent for a moment.

"I don't know exactly who I was," it said. "We are all just memories here, and in time we fade. If you stay here, you will fade too."

"How do I get back?" asked a now terrified Bailey.

"I don't know," said the Other. "But there are many things I do know, and I feel you need to know them too."

***

Scruff was walking back and forth in the alley beside the house. There was no sign of Bailey, and she felt lost. She had been away from him before, but this was different. Usually, even if she didn't know where he was, she knew he was around somewhere. But now she couldn't feel anything. She sat beneath the windowsill and began to cry.

***

Bailey tried jumping back into Dream-Space several times, but each time he just popped right back out again. He was stuck.

"Well," said the Other. "Why don't I tell you the things I know while you work out what to do next?"

"But you said I will start to fade if I stay," said Bailey. "I need to get back."

Baileys Garden in the land of Memories

"It is true," the Other said. "That in time you will fade. All memories fade in time. This is where you are now, the land of memories of things long gone. I once walked in the waking world like you. I too was a Guardian."

"How do you know I'm a Guardian?" asked Bailey.

"It is who you are. It is easy to see," said the Other. "I was a Guardian though I know little more about myself, except that I was loved."

"What do you mean 'was loved'?" asked Bailey.

"Nothing in this universe can ever be wholly created or destroyed," the Other explained. "All things can do is change. I no longer exist in the waking world. I am just a memory. Hardly even a memory now. Soon I will be gone forever."

Bailey looked sad. The Other smiled.

"But it's OK. It's what is supposed to happen. You see, the universe is built on change. Everything must change. Sometimes those changes might seem sad. But change is necessary. Because if things never change, your world would become like this one. Just slowly fading memories. Do you understand?"

Bailey said nothing for some time; as you know, he is quite an intelligent cat really, and now that he had something to think about, the fear dropped from him.

"You said, '*nothing is ever created or destroyed*,'" Bailey was speaking as much to himself as the other, "but then you said your memory will fade and you will not exist. That's a contradiction."[4]

"A-ha well spotted," said the Other. "It's actually perfectly correct and merely seems contradictory."

"Could you explain?" asked Bailey.

"Very well," said the Other. "Imagine in the waking world, I moved a stone, just that. What if a human being trips over that stone long after I have been forgotten? What if, in tripping, he finds some of that 'money' they are always so interested in? So that human goes home and is happy and gives his cat some extra love and affection. Now this cat, who is usually quite naughty with birds and mice, decides to be good."

The 'other' paused, allowing his words to sink in. When Bailey nodded, he continued.

"Already, you can see how much difference the smallest thing can make. But consider. What if a bird lives that the naughty cat would have otherwise eaten? What if it spies a monster loose on the Charnwood and tells a cow, who tells a friendly fox, who passes the message on to the Guardians, who take care of the monster? So that monster doesn't eat a human boy, who grows up and so forth. The whole world is different just because I moved a little stone. Every single thing we do affects everything else. We can never truly be gone. Even if we are forgotten by everyone, the whole

---

[4] (If you're not sure what a contradiction is, try asking an adult, I'm busy telling the story.)

world would be a very different place if we had never been in it."

"Yes," said Bailey, nodding slowly. "I think I see. It's... it's wonderful."

The Other smiled.

"Always remember, even the smallest of us can change the universe."

"Funny," said Bailey. "Shadow used to say that all the time."

The Other put its head to one side. "Tell me about Shadow," it said.

"Well, she lives next door," said Bailey.

Just then a noise arose like a wispy wail of a cry but coming from several directions all at once.

"We haven't got long," said the Other. "If you're going to make it home, now is the time."

***

Scruff was crying quietly. She felt sick, dizzy, and lost without Bailey. A few feet away under a bush two tiny figures watched her intently.

"We should go and see if we can help," whispered one.

"The last time one of us tried to help, she was thrown in the dungeons," said the second. "Her Majesty will do terrible things to us if we help."

"She's already done terrible things to us, don't you understand that?" said the first and it marched quietly out, stood before Scruff, and coughed politely.

Scruff blinked and through the tears, she could see, what at first glance, appeared to be a little Fairy. But then Scruff noticed its nose was a bit long and its ears stuck out just a tiny amount. Though it was a perfectly pretty face, it wasn't as 'perfectly symmetrical' as the other Fairies she had met. And instead of a beautiful gown, it was wearing a dress of patchwork rags. To top it all, Scruff noticed it had no wings.

"I'm sorry," said Scruff. "I didn't see you there. How can I help?"

"Actually," said the little creature. "It is we who hope to help you."

***

Bailey was scared now, really scared. Around him, things were moving, strange nightmare shapes of people, animals, birds, fish, and weird mixtures of them all. They were slowly creeping and crawling towards him.

"They are memories," said the Other. "They are drawn to you. You're real. You can remember them. They are scared of being forgotten for they never learnt the things I have taught you in life: and they can learn nothing now."

Bailey looked around, judging how long he had before they got to him.

"What happens if they reach me?" he asked.

"They will weigh you down, and you won't be able to leave," replied the Other. "In time, you will become another fading memory."

Bailey began to panic. The shapes were creeping up the path by the house. They were oozing over the fence, which leads onto the road. Slithering under the bushes leading to the next block of houses.

"Think!" said the Other. "How did you get here?"

"I was in the graveyard," said Bailey. "I was trying to Dream-Walk home."

"Graveyards are where humans go to remember those who have gone," said the Other. "It's where the world of memories and the waking world are closest."

Without a moment's thought, Bailey leapt back into the graveyard. The stones shone out black against the white grass, and from the ground, transparent grey hands reached out to grab him. The wailing was getting louder as Bailey searched for the spot he had entered Dream-Space and all around him the shapes moved in closer.

***

"What do you mean?" asked Scruff. "How can you help me? Do you know what's happened to Bailey?"

"Bailey?" asked the first of the little creatures. "No... no, I'm sorry we don't. We have come to give you news of Shadow. My name is Mai, I'm a Pixie."

***

Bailey was running in circles. Twisted shadowy forms were closing in, some looking almost like humans or animals. Some distorted nightmare shapes where memories had run together. Human shapes with too many heads or not enough legs. Cats that had many eyes, legs, tails, and claws. Dogs as large as wolves and foxes with teeth like knives.

***

"Look," said Scruff. "I want to hear about Shadow, of course, I do. But right now, I need to find Bailey."

"I saw him in the graveyard," said Mai. "He was smelling the ground on the far side. Then we lost sight of him."

"Show me where," said Scruff. "There's no time to lose."

The Pixies jumped on her back, and the fluffy mess leapt off into the night.

It was pitch dark in the graveyard, but the Pixies guided her true and, in a minute, they were standing where Bailey had disappeared.

***

Bailey was about to lose hope when a scent caught him. He backed up and there it was again. It was the unmistakable smell of Scruff, with all his willpower he slipped into Dream-Space.

Pop!

He was lying in the damp grass at Scruff's feet. Scruff licked his face and snuggled up to him.

"Oh, thank the stars," said Scruff, "I thought I had lost you. Let's get you home."

"Wait," said Bailey. "Don't Dream-Walk. Not here, trust me."

Together they walked back to the small hole in the fence. Scruff climbed through followed closely by the Pixies. Bailey turned back one last time looking into the mist.

"I will remember you," Bailey said.

But the damp night seemed to swallow his words, and he went home.

***

Bailey and Scruff sat in the front room getting warm. The Pixies sat nearby, looking around the flat with interest.

"Reminds me of my old home," said Mai, "If my old home had been made for giants."

"So what have I missed?" Bailey asked.

"They say they have news of Shadow," said Scruff.

"What news?" cried Bailey.

"It was a friend of ours called Nim who wrote the message on your cat-door-thing," said Mai. "Alas, she was caught and is now in a dungeon."

Bailey shook his head. "I'm sorry," he said. "Can we start at the beginning? Who are you, and where do you come from?"

"I'm Mai," said the little Pixie. "My silent friend here is Tai, and we come from Fayre."

Bailey and Scruff jumped to their feet.

"You don't need to worry about us," said Tai, his voice was timid and his eyes downcast. "We're not Fairies anymore."

"What do you mean?" asked Bailey.

"In Fayre, anyone who doesn't meet the Queen's standard for how a 'Fairy' should look. Like my friend Mai here…" said Tai, pointing to his friend.

"Or anyone who argues or questions the Queen's decisions and policies. Like my friend Tai here," said Mai. "Is removed from Fairy society and has their wings removed," said Tai.

"It is the law that all such people are traitors and are to be banished, or used as slaves," said Mai. "The word Pixie has become an insult in our land, for those who are the lowest of the low."

Tai looked at his feet. Scruff and Bailey were both shocked.

"What happened to you, then?" asked Scruff "What terrible crime did you commit?"

"Me?" said Mai. "Can't you see? My nose is too wide, and my ears stick out."

"What?" said Bailey. "WHAT?"

"If you don't look perfect in the Queen's eyes," said Mai. "That's treason too."

"That's terrible," said Scruff. "Why doesn't anyone do something?"

"Tai tried, and they cut off his wings," said Mai. "Our friend Nim tried and was made a slave. But even then, she tried to help you and has been thrown in the dungeons."

"And what's happened to Shadow?" asked Bailey, his imagination running riot.

"They caught her as she leapt over a stream," said Tai. "By making the Fayre door appear right in the middle of it as she jumped. Now she's locked in the lowest dungeon of the Seelie Court in the Castle-city of Fayre."

"But why?" cried Scruff, "What for?"

"For daring to speak against the Queen's wishes at your hearing," said Mai, "and for what you did in rescuing those Brownies. Though that's not how the story is told in the city. They say that on Shadow's orders, you attacked an innocent group of Fairies."

Bailey growled low, making not only the Pixies but Scruff look up.

"We are going to rescue Shadow," he said. "We are going to free the Pixies, and we are going to make sure this Queen can never harm another creature again... Even if it means war.

Chapter 8
The Gathering

Scruff sat on a rock watching the moon as it slowly passed. The rock was ancient, used by the people of the Charnwood for hundreds of years, maybe thousands. It was known as 'Twenty Steps.' By day, children played on or around it and walkers climbed it. But at night, it was used only by the creatures of the Charnwood. Tonight, Scruff needed peace, quiet and time to think.

***

Under a kilometre away, in the ruins of the Grace Dieu Priory was the most critical meeting the forest had seen in hundreds of years.

At the Centre, Bailey stood with the Chairman, around them were the Cats of Charnwood Forest, the Guardians of the other parishes.

There was a large ginger and white tom from Loughborough, a small bluish Persian from Shepshed and a brown shorthair tabby from Markfield. There were even Guardians from as far away as Cropston and Woodhouse-Eves. Not to mention old Tipsy and Tumble whose parish they were in. Other creatures had gathered there as well. There were Brownies of various ages, sizes and shapes, an assortment of Gnomes, and a whole regiment of armed and armoured Goblins. Besides these, a few Boggarts had come south for the meeting. There was even a shoal of Water Sprites, and to everyone's surprise, a Nymph had turned up. They are a rare sight nowadays as I'm sure you know. Most importantly, there were the two Pixies, Mai, and Tai.

They were waiting for Scruff.

The Ruins of Grace Dieu

Scruff went over the meeting in her mind. It had started the moment the sun had gone down. A leader amongst the Goblins rose and explained how their world had been the great hub of the known universe. They spoke of the old times when Kapul-Tok traded with hundreds of worlds, and through Kapul-Tok travellers from everywhere explored the universe in peace. He told of how they were led to believe that the Elves, their closest friends, were jealous of them. How their goods would disappear, and their colonies were destroyed, and always it seemed to be the Elves' fault. How day by day, their fear grew until eventually there was war. He spoke of the last day when all had been lost. The Guardians had tried to get the two old friends to make peace but even that had failed.

"On that last day, there was no peace left to find. We would not risk giving in to a single demand of the Elves," said the Goblin, "and they would risk giving into none of ours. I can't blame them. War changes you. After that, we ordered all of our pools to be covered and cut ourselves off from the universe to await the answer to the riddle."

As the Goblin said those last words, it looked long and hard at Bailey and Scruff, then smiled sadly and turned away.

Next up was WhooWhee, the Brownie elder who told of what they had overheard many years ago. That the Fairies were behind the war, whispering in the ears of the Goblins and the Elves, making them mistrust and eventually hate each other.

The Pixies were questioned again and again. They now sat exhausted as answering questions was tiring work. When all had been said and examined and debated, it was evident that there was only one way to get Shadow back and to stop the Fairies from their insane plan to make all worlds like their own.

They would have to go to Fayre, to the Seelie Court itself. After this, the Fairies and Pixies would have a choice, to co-exist in peace or be cut off from the other worlds forever.

Unfortunately, it was clear that they couldn't do it alone. Had all of the Guardians and Goblins, the Boggarts and Brownies, the Gnomes and the Nymph set off that moment, they would likely fail. For the Fairies had both enormous strength, (considering their size, you may remember one was able to hold Scruff up by her tail,) and of course, they could fly.

They needed the Elves, and there was only one who could reach them. Only one of all the creatures gathered had the skill to Dream-Walk through solid objects. Long ago, the Elves had covered the lake, which was their entrance to Kapul-Tok. The thought of having to jump into Dream-Space while underwater, terrified Scruff, but there was no one else. The Chairman had said that the decision was hers.

***

The east was starting to lighten by the time Scruff came out of her thoughts. In a few hours, the Humans would be up and about. It was time for her to make a choice. For a kind and loyal kitten like Scruff, however, there was no choice. Not really.

She walked back to the priory, feeling the cold damp of the forest floor against her paws, smelling the mossy air, and wondering if it would be for the last time. The meeting quietened to a hush as Scruff reappeared, all ears eyes and noses were on her.

"Tonight, at sundown," she said. "Let me rest 'til then."

The Chairman nodded, Scruff walked behind a tree and moments later was back at home.

She leapt out of Dream-Space right at the foot of the bed, jumped up on her sleeping human and cried out loudly before licking Kirsty's face. Kirsty slowly woke. Her eyes were full of sleep dust and her cheeks were wet from Scruff's kisses. She raised her head and looked at the time.

"Oh Willow," Kirsty said. "It's too early… I'll be up to feed you soon."

With that Kirsty lay down and curled up, Scruff was having none of it. She cried and licked and walked all over Kirsty until eventually, Kirsty got up and sleepily walked to the kitchen.

"Here you go," Kirsty said as she opened a fresh pouch and squeezed the contents into Scruff's bowl. "Can I go back to sleep now?" But to Kirsty's surprise, Scruff wasn't interested in the food.

She followed Kirsty around and cried and rubbed herself up against Kirsty's legs. Kirsty started to become quite concerned.

"What's wrong?" asked Kirsty, as she picked Scruff up and carried her into the front room. Here she took out Scruff's comb and gave her a good grooming.

"Oh, I have such a surprise for you tomorrow," said Kirsty as Scruff rolled onto her back. "I'm sure you're going to love it."

By the time Bailey got home, Kirsty was fast asleep on the chair, and Scruff was fast asleep on her lap.

***

The evening was coming in when Scuff finally left Kirsty's side. While Kirsty was making dinner and preparing for her favourite TV show, and Bailey was eating his dinner, Scruff crept out into the back garden. As she approached the pond, a Goblin stepped out from under the bush. It was wearing a smart if old-fashioned waistcoat, shirt, and tie. It bowed to Scruff as she got close.

"Good evening," it said. "I am Dzukaluke."

"I've heard that name before, haven't I?" Scruff said. "I can't quite remember…"

"It will come back to you I'm sure," said the Goblin smiling, which made its two front teeth protrude even further and its pointy ears stick out until it looked very rat-like indeed.

"Now all you have to do is jump in the pond, make sure you're completely underwater and WISH to be in Kapul-Tok."

Scruff nodded and looked into the pond, but she was too scared to move.

"It will be nightfall soon," said the Goblin anxiously. "If you're going to go, it has to be now."

Taking a deep breath, Scruff leapt into the pond with a splosh. A moment later, Kirsty looked out of the window to see what all the noise was about, but the garden was empty.

***

The world seemed to spin around Scruff. Down was suddenly up, and she splashed and spluttered as she broke the surface of the water and pulled herself out. Thankfully, the pool on the Kapul-Tok side was no deeper than it had been in Kirsty's garden.

Scruff found herself in a smallish cave with a smooth floor. At the far end, a tunnel stretched out of view. The cave was well-lit. Around the walls and ceilings, little gemstones of every colour glowed with a light of their own. Had Scruff looked upon the cave in happier circumstances she would have thought it the most beautiful thing imaginable.

Looking back into the pool, she could see the fading evening sky of her own world, and as she turned away from it, a tear left her eye.

She was starting to head towards the tunnel when a gentle splash made her look back. A Goblin was climbing out of the pool wearing a long, red, and white striped swimming costume, and carrying a bag. The Goblin disappeared behind a large boulder and a moment later returned dressed in suit and tie.

"Oh, it's you, Dzukaluke," said Scruff.

"Welcome to Kapul-Tok," said Dzukaluke as they started to walk down the tunnel. "Ghaz'on speaks highly of you, and I wanted to thank you personally for my child's rescue."

"Of course," said Scruff, "that's where I heard your name from, Ghaz'on spoke about you often. You're Ghaz'on's mother, aren't you?"

"Um no," said Dzukaluke "I'm Ghaz'on's parent. The little darling told me about your world's obsession with calling half of you one thing and the other half another. We don't do that here."

"Ok… um sorry," said Scruff, "It is difficult for me. We tend to call people him or her, and for you, I have to say 'it', which in our world is quite insulting."

"Please explain," Dzukaluke said.

"Well, if I was talking to someone, and I was in our world," Scruff explained, "I might say 'I popped round, and she or he made me some dinner.' But with you, I would have to say, 'I popped round, and *it* made me some dinner.' And in our world, you shouldn't call someone 'it', we use that word for things, not people."

"Ah well, that's easily fixed," Dzukaluke replied. "Since Ghaz'on came back, we have been sending scouts through some of the older pools into your world and discovered that many humans think as we do. They have invented many words to make up for this, and our favourites are the 'Z' ones."

Scruff looked totally blank and had no idea what Dzukaluke was talking about. Dzukaluke chuckled.

"So, to use your example," Dzukaluke continued. "You could say 'I went round to zir place for tea and while I was there, zie made me dinner all by zimself.' What do you think?"

Scruff pondered this for a while.

"It sounds very strange to my ears, but if it's what your people would prefer, I will do my best to respect it."

As they walked, the tunnel ahead seemed to curve upwards, steeper, and steeper and yet Scruff found that no matter how steep it looked, it never felt like going uphill. Other tunnels opened up on the left and right, but Dzukaluke kept them going more or less straight on.

The tunnel became wider and wider until eventually, Scruff noticed the ceiling had gone and high above were wisps of clouds and what looked like a very pale moon in a greyish sky. They had reached the Goblin city of Kapul-Tok. It wasn't quite what Scruff had expected.

Kapul-Tok, whether you think of it as a kingdom, a land, a world or even a universe; whatever you would like to call it, its, from our point of view… inside out.

Our world is, to put it simply, a massive lump of rock in endless space. There are lots of other chunks of rock floating in the emptiness of space, but mostly it's just empty space.

Kapul-Tok, on the other hand, is a vast empty space inside endless rock. There are other empty spaces out there like there are planets here, but mostly it's just continuous solid rock.

Yes, I know, it's hard to imagine.

***

Scruff felt like she was standing at the bottom of a large bowl. All around her, the ground curved upwards, disappearing somewhere above.

Dzukaluke explained that far above them, the ground joined up again and that floating in the middle was not a moon or even a sun but a magnificent crystal like the ones that lit the tunnels.

"Back in the days of the great friendship between Alfhiem and Kapul-Tok," said Dzukaluke, "we Kapul's mined many of the gems you see lighting the tunnels. The Elves, in particular, loved them and traded them with us.

"Occasionally we would find huge ones, as big as houses. The Elves put that one up there to light all of Kapul-Tok."

Scruff followed Dzukaluke through the city. The houses were small and cramped together. The narrow streets all seemed to curve upwards, but just as before, it never really felt like she was walking uphill. After a while, Dzukaluke stopped and pointed to a large building some way above them. Scruff looked up at it in much the same way you might look down on a distant house from the top of a hill. Even from here, it seemed a mighty palace, and she could make out light streaming from many windows.

"That is where we are going," said Dzukaluke. "There is much for you to learn before you attempt to reach Alfhiem."

When they were over halfway there, Scruff looked back and could just about make out the tunnel they had come out of, halfway up the curve of the world behind them. It made her feel quite dizzy, but she took a deep breath and carried on. A little while later, they were standing at the gates of the palace.

The high gold and silver gates of the palace stood wide open, and Goblins of all ages were rushing in and out with paper scrolls, books and charts. Guards were standing by the doors, but they were not particularly scary, and they even bowed to Scruff as she passed

Inside, things were even busier; Goblins rushed back and forth, and Scruff felt quite anxious and wanted very much to run away. A familiar voice called her name, and she saw Ghaz'on squeezing through the crowd, rushing towards her. She ran up to the little Goblin, rubbing herself against its neck. Ghaz'on, in turn, scratched her behind the ears, and though they were not aware, most of the Goblins stopped rushing around and smiled. All but one.

After a time, Dzukaluke interrupted. "I'm afraid I must ask you to come with me, time is short."

Scruff followed Dzukaluke to the council chamber, which seemed strangely empty. A large round table stood in the centre with six chairs and around these, rising up on all sides were hundreds of seats, like you might have seen at a cinema or a football pitch.

Scruff had hardly enough time to take all this in before she was hurried through a small door near the table and into a small chamber. Inside it was organised chaos. A table in the middle was covered in maps, and over them, some older Goblins were looking thoughtfully.

Some of these Goblins had glasses and walking sticks or monocles, and this had the effect of making them look far scarier; like the naughty Goblins in the stories humans tell. A slight cough from Dzukaluke and they looked around. Immediately they saw that Scruff was there, serious frowns broke into looks of joy.

"So, this is to be the answer to the great riddle," said one with a smile.

"The great riddle?" asked Scruff. "It was you, wasn't it? At the meeting last night, you mentioned it there."

"I am Burgh," the Goblin said. "Some of us believe, as I do, that you are the answer we have been waiting many years for. However, time is short, and there is much to do."

For the next few hours, Scruff was shown all of the remaining records and maps of Alfhiem. Much had been lost in the war.

She learnt all she could of the Elves and their customs. Unfortunately, she soon learnt that language might be a problem. The Elves used to understand Cat and Goblin well enough, but if they still spoke it, nobody knew. The Goblins knew nothing of the language of the Elves (it being impossible for the Goblins to pronounce).

The pool she would emerge in was a mighty lake on the Alfhiem side and was a good two or three miles from the Elven city. In the days before the war, it had been a quiet place of farming and learning with libraries and people dedicated to gentle study. They said that during the war, it had become a place of metal and rock and weapons. There was no guarantee the

Elves were still there. Or if they were, what they would be like?

A bell sounded, and everyone started heading out into the council chamber.

"But I still don't understand about this riddle business," said Scruff.

"No need to fret," said Burgh. "It's all about to be made clear."

***

The chamber was filled to overflowing with Goblins of all ages and sizes. As Scruff went in, the Goblins began clapping. Scruff felt quite scared until she realised that this was a good thing. Burgh stood by his seat at the council table and addressed the crowd.

"I believe," said Burgh, "as do most of the council, that the riddle has been answered, and we now have the chance to restore the glory of Kapul-Tok. But before we lend our aid, a tally must be taken as is our custom."

"NO!" From the other side of the council chamber, a Goblin stood in the smartest of clothes and looked down on Scruff with a sneer.

"For hundreds of years," the Goblin said. "We have kept to ourselves and stayed safe. We must remain as we have."

Burgh was about to reply when the main doors opened, and in came the oldest Goblin Scruff had yet seen. It was weathered and wrinkled, with tufts of white hair sticking out of its ears. But it still had a keen look in its eyes.

"People," it said. "Listen not to the words of Kar'ack. Few of us are old enough to remember the war, but I am the only one of you who remembers how things were before. The Elves were a proud and peaceful people. More skilled than us in many areas, they taught us much, and we taught them much in return. We called them friends.

"Then things changed, mistrust, doubt, fear and finally war. I remember those days, and I remember the Fairies, always the bearers of evil tidings. If what we have learnt is true, this Guardian IS the answer to the riddle."

"Nonsense!" cried Kar'ack, "You are NOT a member of the council. You have no place here."

"Tell us Kar'ack," said the old one, looking Kar'ack in the eye, "What do you have to lose through peace? Afraid of competition? Have you not had a monopoly on most of our markets for long enough?"

Kar'ack glanced around anxiously at the looks of anger from the enormous crowd.

"That is my opinion as a member of the council," Kar'ack said at last. "If all of you are against me, so be it."

"I asked the old one here today," Said Burgh as he stood, "as an original witness to the riddle and the only one who can speak the words true."

"On the last day," the old one said, "the head of the Kapul-Tok council and the Elven Queen met on the Charnwood. It was the last chance to find peace.

"Hours went by, but there was no peace to be found for there was no trust left. In the final moments, a Whisp appeared, and it spoke, saying,

> 'Many years must pass old friends,
> Before this evil, makes its end.
> When innocence is saved at cost,
> Of valiant heart and all seems lost.
> When the smallest ones are kind and brave.
> You will unite, and evil will fade.'

"Those are the true words."

The old one was helped to a seat, and Burgh nodded in thanks before turning back to the crowd.

"This Kitten," said Burgh, "the smallest of the Guardians of whom our old tales tell, has shown herself to be both kind and brave.

"She saved one of our smallest: Ghaz'on. Her valiant master was captured by the Fairies while looking for Ghaz'on. And if that is not enough, we learn now that it was the Fairies that started the war. The riddle is answered. Who is with us?"

The chamber erupted into applause. Before Scruff knew what was happening, she was being bustled into a tunnel and to a remote lake.

***

The journey was long, and Scruff was quite exhausted by the time she reached the lakeside. She lay down on her side and panted. Some Goblins brought her a bowl of clear water, which she drank thankfully, and a bowl of fish, which she nibbled on. When she was well-rested, she got up and had a good look around. What she saw sent her running back into the tunnel.

The cavern was vast, but the lake inside it was even bigger. From the shore where Scruff had lain, it spread not only far back into the gloom, but up the cave walls and across much of the ceiling. Scruff found it hard to be in there. She kept getting the feeling a colossal wave was about to fall on her.

Dzukaluke and Ghaz'on had come to see her off, and they tried to calm her down. When she had plucked up the courage, she looked into the lake. There was no light coming out of it, not the slightest flicker of star or moonlight. But of course, it was covered over on the Alfhiem side.

"How do we know it's night-time there?" Scruff asked.

"We have records," Dzukaluke said. "We know that when it is midnight in your world, it is early morning in their world."

Dzukaluke gave her a small pod.

"In here is a letter for the Elves. Hopefully, they will understand it. It's up to you now. You know what to do."

"Ok," said Scruff. "Guess there is no time like the present." Scruff held the pod in her mouth and jumped into the lake.

Just as she was going under the surface, she heard a voice shout out "Ghaz'on, NO!" She felt something wrap its little arms around her neck, the pod was knocked from her mouth, and before she knew what was happening, the world turned upside down.

Chapter 9
Alfhiem

Scruff panicked. The water here was colder and deeper. The thing around her neck and the weight of her waterlogged fur was pulling her down. In the shock she had lost some precious air, her lungs were burning.

She tried to calm herself and felt the thing on her back, kicking water. Scruff kicked too, hoping to reach a surface and gasp air. She had forgotten that the pool had been covered on the Alfhiem side. She felt the thing on her back hit the cover and go limp, but at that moment the way into Dream-Space opened before her.

She couldn't remember before whether she breathed when in Dream-Space. It had never occurred to her. She dared not try. Her lungs still burnt, but at least it wasn't getting any worse, and her mind felt calmer.

She guessed now that the thing on her back was Ghaz'on. The silly Goblin must have forgotten that Scruff couldn't jump into Dream-Space with someone wide awake. She hoped Ghaz'on wasn't too hurt. But if not for the bump on the head, they would both be lost.

Sometimes when you dream, you know it's a dream and can have lots of fun and find you have superpowers or go on adventures. Dream-Space works similarly and for similar reasons.

As soon as Scruff entered Dream-Space, the blackness turned to the usual shadowy-greys. It seemed far too bright after the cold dark of the lake. She could see the colossal barrier above them. It went on as far as she could see in every direction. There was no going around it, and so she charged straight towards it.

How she knew what to do, I can't tell you. As you probably know, Scruff is a creature of instinct. She tried to imagine that the barrier was just another sort of door and concentrated on all she had learnt about Alfhiem.

With a quiet pop, she came out of Dream-Space a few feet above the ground. She tumbled through the air but landed on her feet.

Ghaz'on, however, fell to the ground with a thud. Scruff rushed over. Ghaz'on was breathing, but not easily. She rolled the Goblin onto its side, and it started to cough up the water it had swallowed. But it didn't wake up, and there was a large dark bruise on its head.

Scruff looked around. They were on a plain ringed by mountains, and though it was night, the peaks glittered in the light of the moons.

Scruff's jaw dropped down. She remembered the explicit instructions that the Goblins had given her:

'The moon will have begun to set by the time you arrive. Head towards the mountain beneath the moon.'

They had unfortunately forgotten to mention that there were three moons.

She looked around for any clue. The plain was covered with grass that looked blue in the moonlight. (Scruff discovered later that it also looked blue in the daylight. There was a good reason for this... It was blue.) She was unable, however, to see any paths.

The only thing she could think of doing was heading towards one of the moons and hoping for the best. The air was warm and the sky clear, so she made Ghaz'on as comfortable as possible, picked a moon at random and headed towards it.

She almost enjoyed the walk. The air had a clean, wholesome taste and the little streams and tall trees that cropped up here and there reminded her of the Charnwood, (were it not for the enormous wooden monstrosity which covered the whole of the lake).

After a time, she decided to head back. There was no sign of the Elves, and so she decided to check on Ghaz'on and then head out again. She reached the spot on which they had landed, but the Goblin was nowhere to be seen. Scruff tried to calm herself down.

'What would Bailey do if he were here?' she asked herself.

In her imagination, she could imagine him sniffing around for clues, and so she did the same. There was no scent of Ghaz'on except where he had been lying. But there was another smell, a sweet fragrance. Not sweet-but-sickly like the Fairies, this was sweet like the scent of a meadow on a fine day after a light rain.

Where this scent lingered, there were marks on the ground. Not heavy shoe marks of a human or Goblin, but the lightest of marks. The footprints led off towards one of the setting moons, and Scruff began to follow.

One of the moons had almost set before Scruff found the path. Here there was a faint smell of Ghaz'on, as if whatever carried it had put it down for a moment. She hurried along as fast as she could, and there at the valley's mouth, stood the city of the Elves.

As Scruff got closer, she began to see where high walls and battlements had been carved out of the very rock of the mountains. But these were worn and tumbling.

All around, however, well-tended fields were ripe with corn and other foods.

Inside the arch of what had once been a mighty gate, a path ran to a large square. From this direction, Scruff could hear many voices arguing. All around the plaza, beautiful wooden buildings stood and creeping forward she saw the Elves for the first time.

***

Have you ever held up a pearl to the moonlight, and seen the way it almost glows with a creamy white light, broken up with blues and reds and greens as the light ebbs and flows?

This was how the skin of the Elves appeared to Scruff, and she couldn't think of anything more beautiful in all the worlds.

They were tall, easily as tall as Kirsty and their hands were strong with many long fingers for making beautiful things; six fingers on each hand Scruff noticed.

They wore simple clothes, little more than long bags with head and armholes, girt with a slim belt around the waist. Yet on the Elves, they looked like the most elegant garments ever made.

Scruff crept forward until she could hear them talking. The language was more like that of Humans than of Cats or Goblins. Scruff could understand most of it.

They were wondering what to do with the Goblin; some were worried the war was about to start again. Others said the creature must be a spy. Many agreed that it should be locked away and never allowed to leave.

Scruff listened to the discussion while the moons set, and as they did so, the skin of the Elves changed. Now under starlight, they appeared as would a swift river at night, sparkling darkly with white breakers like the crests of waves making up their features.

On the left side of the square, a platform stood with two high-backed chairs. On this, an Elf said that whatever the Goblin was doing there, it was clearly ill, and it needed to be cared for before anyone tried questioning it. This Elf was tall and queenly and by her side sat another whose beard ran down to his waist like a foamy waterfall.

Scruff decided that these were the ones she needed to approach. She jumped down from her hiding place, made her way to the edge of the town square and coughed politely.

At that moment, the sun came over the distant peaks, and the Elves seemed to explode with light. Scruff didn't stick around, half-blinded she ran for cover as, behind her, the light dulled down until each, and every Elf looked like it was sculpted from living ice and lit by a light deep within.

Cats don't take well to sudden bright lights; they prefer to hunt at night. Daytime is for snuggles and endless catnaps (preferably under a hot sun). So, Scruff ran. Her eyes hadn't recovered. She ran deeper into the city and straight into a wooden doorpost. She knew nothing more for some time.

***

Two worlds away, Bailey paced back and forth on the window ledge. The evening was coming in, but there was no word from Scruff and come what may, if she wasn't back by dawn, he would lead the troops to Fayre alone. He could only hope she would meet him in Kapul-Tok or else make it home safely.

Bailey's tummy was in such a knot that he couldn't settle. Behind him, Kirsty was rushing around, polishing the tables and hoovering. But Bailey didn't notice. He just paced back and forwards on the windowsill, watching as the shadows lengthened.

***

Scruff opened one eye carefully. She was in a dimly lit room. As her eyes became attuned, she could see that she was lying on some sort of table. For a moment she was reminded of the vets and got quite worried, but then she noticed she was on lovely warm pillows. On a table across from her was a small bed, and she could just make out Ghaz'on. Leaning over him was an Elf. This one's skin glowed softly as if lit from within by a candle. Apart from a few stray sunbeams, which crept under the door, this was the only light in the room.

As Scruff rubbed the sleep from her eyes, she suddenly remembered why she was there.

"Help me," squeaked Scruff. The Elf turned around, and Scruff saw that its face was old and young at the same time. Though it looked like glass, it had creases and lines like a human face and when it moved not a single crack appeared. Its shape was also clearly more like a human, save for the six fingers, but there was something a little cattish maybe about the way it moved.

"Guardian," it said bowing. "I am Fienel, and I'm here to help you. Fear not, your bruise was only slight."

"How's Ghaz'on?" Scruff asked. The Elf looked at her blankly.

"The Goblin child there," Scruff said. "Its name is Ghaz'on. It's my friend. How is it? Is it ok?"

The Elf's face froze with fear, and it ran out of the room. Scruff leapt from the table and immediately had to lie down for a moment. (If you ever bump your head, you should always be careful getting back up again.)

After a while, she struggled back to her feet and climbed up the table opposite. Ghaz'on looked quite well. The bump on its head had gone down, and it seemed to be in a gentle sleep. Scruff wondered what to do.

'Maybe,' she thought, 'if I can get under the young Goblin, I can Dream-Walk it to safety. It should be easy while it's asleep: but then what? I'm here to get the Elves to trust me. Running away won't help, and I can't think of anywhere better to put Ghaz'on.'

At that moment, the little Goblin opened his eyes.

"Are you ok?" Ghaz'on asked.

"I'm fine," said Scruff. "How about you?"

"I feel kind of sick and hungry and thirsty and shaky," said Ghaz'on.

"It was a foolish thing you did jumping on my back," said Scruff. "It was very nearly the end of us both, and if you hadn't got knocked out, it *would* have been the end of us both."

Ghaz'on looked very sad, and in the end, Scruff couldn't stay cross. She licked the little Goblin's face and nuzzled up.

"It's ok," she said. "We will soon have things sorted."

The door creaked as Fienel returned with two guards.

"There, I told you." Said Fienel. "They are in this together."

"I'm afraid you and your… friend, are under arrest Guardian," one of the guards said. It moved forward to grab Scruff.

Scruff whispered in Ghaz'on's ear that she would be back, leapt under the table and jumped into Dream-Space.

Scruff took her time, although it was as misty as ever, she could see the Elves clearly as if they cast sharper shadows into dream. Stranger still, although time outside seemed to be running as slowly as before, the Elves she passed seemed to turn their heads minutely towards her. It was as if they were aware of her presence.

Soon she was back at the square where she had seen the King and Queen; it was empty now. Upon the stage where the King and Queen had sat, a short path headed up to a tower behind. There was a single guard at the bottom, which Scruff rushed past. Inside was a great hall and at the far end, sat the King and Queen on high thrones. The King was reading books and signing papers, whereas the Queen looked straight at Scruff.

"The Guardian has arrived, my love," the Queen said. The King looked up from his paperwork.

"Where?" he asked.

"Over by the door," said the Queen. "It's hiding in Dream."

"So it is," said the King and then he shouted "Hoy, YOU… GUARDIAN! Come and sit close to us. You will be quite safe. We might be able to see you through the veil of dreams, but we can't stop you from coming and going that way."

The Queen put a large cushion on the floor, close enough for Scruff to talk to them, but far enough away that Scruff felt safe. The words of the King came slowly, but Scruff had no difficulty understanding. She came forward, sniffing everything.

This world was so different that she couldn't make much of the scents, but nothing seemed dangerous.

So, at length, she settled down on the cushion, turning around a few times as cats will and then sat looking towards the King and Queen. Some time passed, and then Scruff remembered she was still in Dream-Space. She quickly moved behind a large stone pillar, and with a thought, she was back in Alfhiem.

"Well met," said the King. "I am King Verum, and this is Queen Tiya." The Queen nodded and smiled.

"We haven't had a visitor from beyond our realm since before the war. I must apologise if we have startled you, but many of the people are scared. Especially as you have managed to get through our barrier with a, well, you brought a…"

"Its name is Ghaz'on," said Scruff. "It is a Goblin child and my friend."

"I see," said the King gravely. "The law says that Goblins and their associates are to be imprisoned. I'm very sorry. I hoped maybe the Goblin forced you, but if it's your friend then the law is clear." The King lifted his arm to summon the guards, but the Queen stopped him.

"Think, my love," she said. "Even if we managed to capture it, a Guardian could escape through Dream anytime it wanted. The Guardians were always the most trusted of advisors. Let it speak."

The King dropped his hand and nodded.

"Tell us your story," the Queen said. "What has brought you all the way here? I see in your face that you are in haste."

Now that it came to it, Scruff didn't know what to say. She was sure asking them to dive straight into another war would not be helpful.

"I… along with my friend Ghaz'on," she said at last, "are the answer to the riddle."

The King's mouth hung open. The Queen's face was impassive, as stern, and as cold as an icicle. Silence hung in the great hall like a grey cloud. Then all in a moment the Queen quite literally beamed a smile that lit the room in a warm pinkish-grey light.

"Yes… yes," the Queen cried, rushing forwards, and picking Scruff up in a hug. "I see the truth of it in your eyes. At last, the riddle is answered."

The King, however, was unmoved.

"This Guardian may be the answer to the riddle," the King said slowly and sternly. "But then it may not. Let it tell its story in full before we pass judgment."

The Queen carried Scruff over to her throne and sat the kitten upon it. Then Scruff told them everything that had happened to them since Shadow had disappeared.

The King and Queen listened intently. When Scruff told them what WhooWhee of the Brownies had said, the Queen gasped. When she told them about Mai and Tai the Pixies, the King thumped his fist on the arm of his throne. Tears like pearls welled up in the corner of his eyes. Elves can be stern in war, but they don't like the thought of innocent creatures being hurt.

When Scruff had finished, the King and Queen were quiet for some time. They stared at each other, and Scruff had the feeling that they were speaking together in their thoughts, just as she and Bailey did. Eventually, it was the King who broke the silence, and for the first time, he smiled and shone with a yellow light, which blended with the pink of the Queen, bathing the hall in a warm orange.

"I must ask you to be patient," said the King, "I no longer doubt you, but I am a cautious old king. We will bring your friend Ghaz'on here and ask him to tell his story, which I'm sure will be the same as yours and all will be fine. In the meantime, we will take care of you. I'm sure you are hungry!" The King called over a guard who bowed low to the King and Queen and even Scruff.

"Take our guest to the kitchen and find something for her to eat," the King ordered.

The Queen smiled and scratched Scruff behind the ears. Then Scruff followed the guard through a small side door and along a short stone passage to the kitchens. The kitchens were not particularly busy at this time of day, and the guard started looking around the pantry.

"I am called Gothrick," said the guard. "What would you like to eat?"

"Do you have any fish?" Scruff asked licking her lips. Gothrick stopped as did everything else in the kitchen.

Someone over the other side gasped and dropped a plate, which shattered the sudden silence.

"You eat…flesh?" asked the guard.

"Yes. I am a cat," said Scruff. "We can't digest much vegetation. Just a little grass now and then when we're feeling poorly."

"I'm afraid we have nothing like that," said the guard. "We are vegetarians."

Scruff was about to tell the guard that it was ok and that she would just have some water if she may.

"What about eggs?" he said. "We have some eggs…"

"Oh, yes, please," said Scruff. "Kirsty let me try hers once. I particularly like the yellow bit."

The guard gently fried two lovely big eggs and Scruff hungrily ate the yellows and even some of the whites. After which she and the guard talked about their own worlds.

Gothrick had been a guard in the castle for over a hundred years. He had a wife, who was a teacher and a farmer, and a daughter who was still barely more than a child, being only twenty-three.

Scruff and Gothrick were soon fast friends, and when the Queen came down to call them back to the throne room, she stood for a few moments watching them talk. Then she smiled and her glow was like the green of new leaves in spring, but the two friends barely noticed.

A little while later, Scruff stood before the King and Queen with Ghaz'on on one side and Gothrick on the other.

"I must apologise," said the King. "I had no idea just how young you or your friend are. It has been a long time since we have seen a Goblin or a Guardian. Your friend Ghaz'on is an admirable and brave creature, if a little reckless." As the King said this, Ghaz'on bowed, and the King chuckled.

"You came here to ask for help," The Queen said, "but please understand we are not prepared for war. The last one almost destroyed us." Scruff stepped forward.

"Your Majesties," she said. "We have no wish for war. Our mission is to get in, rescue Shadow and if possible, broker peace. If not... then we must make sure they can never leave their world. It has all been planned."

"The Fairies will outnumber you, and they have great strength," said the Queen. "However, it's in the air that they are most deadly."

"It was for that very reason I was sent here," said Scruff. "The Goblin council seemed to think you could help with air support."

"Hmm, yes, that's possible," said the King. He looked to the Queen, who smiled and nodded.

"Commander Gothrick," said the Queen. "Please show our guests what we can offer by way of air support."

Gothrick snapped a salute to the King, bowed to the Queen and smartly marched off, beckoning for Scruff and Ghaz'on to follow. At the back of the tower, a long road wound up into the mountains and this they followed. On they went until the sun was starting to fall lower in the sky.

'*I haven't got long left,*' Scruff thought. '*The battle will start, and my brother will be in danger, and I will be too late.*'

***

They had been climbing for some hours when Scruff noticed the sound of singing someway below her. Looking back, she was surprised at how high they had climbed. The top of the King's tower was far below them. Squinting against the sun, Scruff could make out a great many Elves in white armour marching up behind them. Gothrick did not slow down.

Ahead of them, a smooth cliff loomed closer and closer, and Scruff noticed a dark hole, which grew and grew as they approached.

The sky dimmed for a moment as something blotted out the sun. They reached the enormous mouth of the cave, and all in front of Scruff was pitch black.

"This," said Gothrick, "is our idea of air support." He whistled a high note and within the cave, glowing red eyes too numerous to count suddenly shone out, and a moment later the sound of beating wings.

Chapter 10
The Choices of Bailey

Bailey paced back and forth along the windowsill. All night he had watched the garden looking out for Scruff, but there was no word, no message at all. In the east, the sky was lightening, and it was almost time for him to go. As he paced, he worried about a great many things.

Kirsty had gone to bed late. She had spent the day almost ignoring Bailey as she moved furniture and cleaned, but as the evening had turned into night, she had become increasingly worried about Scruff. For the last few hours before bed, she had wandered around the garden and the small roads close by calling for 'Willow.' (Willow was Kirsty's name for Scruff, as I'm sure you remember.)

She even asked the neighbours, but eventually, she had given up and gone to bed. She had lain there for a while stroking Bailey.

"Where is that silly girl?" she had said, stifling a yawn. "I hope she's back soon. It's a big day tomorrow." And with that, she fell into a restless sleep. As soon as Kirsty was dreaming, Bailey had crept back to the window and continued his sleepless watch. That was many hours ago. Now the night was old, and dawn was not far off.

Had any Human visited the garden just then (and I can't think of any good reasons for a human to visit Kirsty's garden in the early hours of the morning), it would have looked peaceful and quiet. From where he was sitting, Bailey could see a Goblin hiding amongst the stones of the rockery in Pippa's garden. Some Pixies hid under the leaves of a young Lily. There was a group of Brownies in a corner looking like a pile of leaves.

In a barrel, a few Water Sprites were hiding. On the lawn, a group of Gnomes looked like a small ring of mushrooms, and on top of the sheds all around, Guardians were waiting. Under the hedge, Bailey's friend Fox was hiding the light of a Nymph, and a group of Boggarts were sleeping on his back.

Far away, a cock crowed, and the Goblins stood up, beckoning that it was time to go.

Bailey could wait for Scruff no longer, the sun had crept over the horizon, and it was too late for his sister to come through. Hoping to see Scruff on the other side, Bailey slunk through the cat flap and headed to the garden. Ahead of him, one by one, the various creatures jumped into the pond and disappeared. Eventually, only Bailey, the Goblin and old Fox remained.

"I'm a little scared," said Bailey.

"You?" said the Goblin. "But you're a Guardian."

"Scruff is the one for rushing off into adventures," said Bailey. "She has called me a 'scaredy-cat' many times."

"Nonsense," said Fox. "It was you who took charge against the Fairies up by the monastery, and I know you will sort things out and get Shadow back. I will stay here to let your sister know what has happened if she comes. Though I'm sure, you will see her before I do."

"However, if you want to back out," said the Goblin, "now is the time to say." Anger briefly flashed in Bailey's eyes.

"They have hurt my friends, they have hurt my sister, and they have taken our teacher," he said, Oh, I wouldn't miss this."

Bailey winked at the old fox and leapt into the water.

Bailey had never liked water much. He coughed and spluttered as he pulled himself out of the pool on the Kapul-Tok side and shook himself dry. Some nearby Boggarts and Gnomes had to run away as water flew everywhere.

Around the small cave, two hundred Goblins in full armour stood to attention as they tried to hide the smirks that crossed their faces. Watching a legendary Guardian shivering and shaking is not something you see every day.

There was no time for a tour of Kapul-Tok. As soon as Bailey had stopped shaking, Burgh rushed up and guided him towards the far exit.

"We've had no word from Scruff or Ghaz'on," Burgh said, "but we have found and uncovered the old pool which leads to Fayre…"

As they went on, Burgh explained that from the old maps, it seemed the pool would come out in a small lake in the middle of a forest many miles from the city of Fayre. From there, a short walk south would bring them to a road that wound southeast to the Castle City of Fayre and the Seelie Court of the Queen itself.

Bailey worried that things must have changed in the hundreds of years since the war ended. He asked the Pixies if they would have a look. Mai and Tai scratched their heads and eventually admitted they didn't recognise anything on the map. But Burgh was sure they wouldn't have any trouble finding the castle. It would be the biggest, tallest, and indeed the brightest thing they would ever see.

"It's like a tower of pearl and silver stretching up into the sky," Burgh said as they walked, "even at night you can see it for miles around."

For the next two hours, Bailey and the others followed Burgh through many tunnels that twisted and turned. Some were bigger and brighter, some smaller with barely any light at all. At one point they went through a large cavern filled with mushrooms. There were many caverns like this throughout Kapul-Tok, as the Goblins loved mushrooms almost as much as they loved fish.

The Gnomes seemed horrified, and poor old Burgh was beside himself apologising for bringing them that way.

Suddenly all of the Gnomes started squeaking with laughter. When everyone had calmed down, they explained to the poor Goblin that while Gnomes may look like mushrooms or toadstools, they were not in fact mushrooms or fungi, and they didn't mind at all what the Goblins ate. It was a few minutes before Burgh was able to see the funny side; the Gnomes, however, were giggling for a long while after.

***

Eventually, the tunnels ended, and they reached the pool to Fayre. Groups of Goblins were still removing the large metal sheets they had used to cover it over. The water below was deep and dark and yet despite the lack of light, the water sparkled.

While the work of uncovering the pool went on, the Goblins fed all of the different creatures with food and drink that was suitable to them.

(Interestingly the Gnomes quite liked to munch on some large lettuce leaves, which somewhat resembled the Brownies. The Brownies quite enjoyed some steamed mushrooms, which goes to show just how crazy the universe can be at times.)

Bailey had eaten before leaving, but even so, he munched nervously on some fish. It was while he was munching that he noticed a Goblin crying by the pool.

Tears as big as peas were rolling down its long pointy nose and dropping with a quiet splash into the pool. Bailey walked up to the Goblin and introduced himself.

"You're Bailey?" the Goblin said, "The same Bailey who looked after my child when Ghaz'on fell into your world?"

"That's me," said Bailey, "What's wrong?"

"I'm Dazukaluke, Ghaz'on's parent. Ghaz'on leapt onto Scruff's back as she jumped into the pool to Alfhiem. I don't know what's happened to them. They say that pool is covered on the Alfhiem side. What if they drowned?"

Bailey had never stopped to think for a moment that anything serious could have happened to Scruff, and just thinking about it for a moment made him want to cry as well. But he is, as I have said many times before, a very calm and thoughtful kitten. And so, as Shadow had taught him, he acknowledged his fears but kept on thinking.

"I don't know what's happened," Bailey said, "but I do know that if there is anything Scruff can do to protect Ghaz'on, she will do it. For now, we must hope for the best."

Dazukaluke nodded, and Bailey nuzzled up against the Goblin for a moment before turning back to the gathering.

"Ah Bailey," said Burgh. "It's almost sunrise, on the Fayre side. The days there are only twelve hours long. So, once you're through and the sun rises, we won't be able to send anyone to you for six hours."

Bailey nodded; he knew what this meant. Even If Scruff did get help from Alfhiem, they were on their own. True they could retreat to Kapul-Tok if things got too bad. But once the Fairies were aware of them, they wouldn't get a second chance. Taking a deep breath, Bailey turned to the crowd.

"CAN I HAVE YOUR ATTENTION?" Bailey cried. "The time has come. It is up to us to rescue Shadow and stop this evil from spreading. Nymph, you're with me. After we jump in the rest of you come in this order. Pixies, Brownies, Goblins, Boggarts, Sprites; and then the other Guardians. Ready? Go."

***

After the first trip, Bailey was able to anticipate the way the world would flip upside down and the awful feeling in his stomach, which went with it. It was like he had been thrown up in the air unexpectedly.

As he leapt out in Fayre, he resisted shaking for fear someone would hear. Beside him, the Nymph floated up as dry as dry can be.

"Something's wrong," said Bailey. "This place doesn't smell right."

Inside Bailey's mind, the Nymph's voice echoed, *'I feel it also. Nature itself is imprisoned. I hear the earth crying out for freedom.'*

Behind them, the other creatures were climbing out, and as they did, Bailey took in his surroundings. The pond was perfectly round with a bricked ledge instead of a natural bank. In the centre, a fountain sprayed water into the air. Around this was a path with little Fairy-sized benches and around these were beautiful flowerbeds full of vivid colours. The pond was in a perfectly square field of emerald-green grass. As Bailey looked around, he discovered that this was just one of hundreds of perfectly identical meadows. The forest was utterly destroyed.

In the distance, rising up like a mountain was the city-castle of Fayre. It was the biggest thing Bailey had ever seen, but it was no longer a tower of pearl and silver.

The monstrosity they saw on the horizon was pink, very pink. It wasn't the delicate pink you see in a blossom or a rose, but a hard unnatural pink. A sickly-sweet smell invaded his nostrils, reminding him of the encounter at the Calvary. He found it hard to hold in a sneeze.

'*The flowers, the grass,*' Nymph thought, '*It's all wrong, not real…*'

Bailey crept forward and stepped on the grass. The Nymph was right. It felt wrong, rubbery. By now the army had all come through, just in time as the sun rose. They could go back, but there would be no help from Kapul-Tok for at least six hours. Bailey called everyone together.

"Mai, Tai," he said. "What the heck is going on here?"

"We did tell you we didn't recognise anything on that map," said Mai.

"Everything for a hundred miles around the castle is fake," said Tai. "The Queen hates nature. She says it's unpredictable, dirty, and muddy. She wants everything she sees from her high tower in the castle to look perfect. So the grass is something from your world called 'Astroturf.' The flowers are something called 'plastic.' Every day, groups of Pixies are forced to walk around spraying everything with that awful perfume."

Hearing this, the Brownies gasped, and the Gnomes grumbled. Of all the creatures there, they were closest to the earth and needed it like we need food and water. Bailey was quiet for some time as he pondered what to do next.

"Mai, how many of the Pixies and Fairies will turn to our side, do you think?" he asked.

"All of the Pixies to be sure," said Mai, "but the Fairies? I don't know. The poorer ones maybe, but other than that I just don't know."

"Ok, Mai, can you and Tai go and get the Pixies?" asked Bailey.

"We can spread the word so they will be ready," said Tai, "but if they all came here in a group, the game would be up."

"There are other Pixie settlements," said Mai, "but it will be next to impossible to get them here undetected."

"Ok," said Bailey. "Just get to the ones near the city ready and tell them to wait for the right moment."

"When will that be?" asked Tai.

"I don't know," said Bailey. "When the Fairies are concentrating on us, I guess. Before you go, what do you know about the castle and its defences?"

"I'm afraid we don't know much," said Mai. "We come from a village far away. The only time I was in the castle was as a prisoner. The guards are armed and armoured, and there seemed to be a lot of them… that's all we know."

Bailey nodded with a sigh, and the two Pixies went on their way.

"We need to know the castle's defences," said Bailey to the waiting crowd around him. "How many guards, towers, gates and all that stuff."

'I could go, as fast as a whisper,' said the voice of the Nymph in their minds.

"Could you keep your glow down? So they wouldn't see you?" Bailey asked, hopefully.

'No,. I'm afraid not,' the Nymph thought in reply.

Bailey paced back and forth, trying to decide what to do. He needed information badly.

"Excuse me, Sonny Jim," said one of the Boggarts. There were several of the creatures, who were about seven inches high. They were green-skinned with big muscles and big fat noses. Some wore kilts, some wore trousers, and some wore armour made of old pots and pans.

"I dinna ken if yous aware tha ouse Boggarts are masters of disguise?" the Boggart said.

Bailey had started to laugh but suddenly stopped. Right in front of Bailey's eyes, the Boggart's arms became thinner and whiter. Then its nose shrunk, its bald head grew long blonde hair, and its kilt turned into a beautiful dress. Two wings sprouted from its back, and suddenly where the Boggart had stood, a Fairy seemed to be twirling around. Only the half-green, half-blue eyes gave him away as a Boggart.

"Wow," said Bailey. "Can you all do that?"

"Aye we can," said the Boggart, "but as youse can tell, our voices dinna change tha' much."

"It will have to do," said Bailey, "Nymph… say do you have a name? I can't keep calling you 'Nymph'."

'Yes,' the Nymph thought, 'but you couldn't possibly pronounce it. Just calling me Nymph will be fine.'

"Ok, you go with the Boggarts and hide near the castle," said Bailey. "When the Boggarts have got something to report, they can tell you, and you rush back here."

Moments later, what appeared to be a group of Fairies were skipping along the road to the castle, while arguing about the best way to scare an old miser into spending his money: but that's Boggarts for you.

Bailey called all the others together.

"We're going to give the Boggarts and Pixies an hour's head start," he said. "Then we will make our way slowly but surely towards the castle. Hopefully, we will receive news before we get too close."

Bailey's army nodded in approval.

"Guardians, you create a perimeter around us," Bailey ordered. "Stay hidden and warn us if anything comes close. Water Sprites, stay in the pool. If we need to get word to Kapul-Tok, you're our best bet."

"There is a pipe here feeding the fountain and another taking the extra water away, so the pond doesn't overflow," said one of the Water Sprites in her bubbly little voice. "We could follow it. You never know where it might lead."

Bailey thought hard, there were seven Water Sprites in all, and he didn't like the thought of any of them being put in danger.

"Ok," he said at last. "Six of you explore the pipe, see what you can do, but don't take any risks. The rest of us will head off in an hour. And I will need one of you here to contact Kapul-Tok."

He didn't know it, but every creature there was looking up to him at that moment, even the other Guardians. On the outside, Bailey seemed strong and fearless; inside, his tummy was churning.

'Where are you Scruff,' he thought, *'I've never needed you more, you scruffy mess.'*

But Scruff was two worlds away.

***

Some way away and a little time later, Mai and Tai wandered down one of the many perfectly paved paths arguing in hushed whispers.

"We should head for the outcast village," said Mai, "We can be there in a couple of hours, they are bound to help."

"But by the time we get to the city, the battle will have started," said Tai. "We should head for the slave quarters of the castle. I'm sure we will get lots of support."

"But what if we don't?" said Mai. "Late help is better than no help. Besides Bailey might win by diplomacy."

"You know how fanatical that Queen is. It's more likely the battle will be lost before we get there!" said Tai.

"We haven't been to the capital for years," said Mai. "We have no idea what's happening there. We would be walking blindly into danger."

Tai was about to reply when from some way up ahead they heard the sound of two other voices arguing. They were clearly Pixies. They were dressed, if you can call it dressed, in the worst sort of rags. One had a dress, which was practically all patches, and even this had horrible holes in it. Its hair hung down in lank locks, and its face was so dirty it was hard to tell what bit was what. Though it still had the bright eyes of Fairy kind.

The other was shorter and apart from the eyes didn't look very fairylike at all. It had better clothes, a pair of faded black trousers with threadbare knees and a scruffy blazer under which it wore a string vest. They were carrying huge bottles on their backs with which they would spray the plastic flowers as they passed. Mai and Tai wrinkled up their noses, recognising that horrible cheap, sickly-sweet perfume.

"Careful where you spray," said the first Pixie.

"Watch where you stand," said the other.

"Ughhh this stuff smells so bad I can hardly think," said the first.

"Shh," said her companion. "It's saying things like this that got you turned into a Pixie."

Mai and Tai hid behind a plastic bush and waited until the newcomers were level with them and then called them over.

"Psst," said Mai. "Over here."

The other Pixies jumped with surprise and stared at Mai and Tai for a few moments. Then the one in the patchwork dress came over cautiously.

"We can't talk to you," she said. "If we're caught, we will be beaten."

"Not if we have anything to do with it," said Tai. "We have come to take the city and put things right. We have been beaten and treated as slaves for long enough. We need to gather as many Pixies to the cause as possible… can you help?"

The short Pixie leaned forward and whispered.

"Even if we could gather all the Pixies and Pixie sympathisers together there would not be enough to overthrow the castle," he said.

Mai smiled. "I don't want to say too much just in case," she whispered, "but we have been outside the realm of Fayre and brought back help. The Guardians have returned."

The astonished Pixies introduced themselves smiling.

"I'm Chai," said the tall one in the patchwork dress. "My village is close to here. We can start raising help there."

"I'm Joi," said the shorter one. "I don't really want to get involved myself. I'm deathly scared of. the Queen

But I own a boat on the Caliburn River. You're welcome to borrow it."

"The Caliburn?" cried Mai. "We're close to the Caliburn? That leads right past the outcast village. I could get there in no time."

A while later, they reached a crossroads and took the left-hand road. Ahead of them, a bridge crossed a broad, swift river to an island. The bridge was ornate with carved statues of the Fairy Queen standing on either side of the entrance. The near bank was as clean and utterly fake as the rest of Fayre. But here, the fakery ended.

The further bank was all-natural, overgrown with trees and bushes, which almost glowed in the afternoon light. There were leaves and stalks of dark green and dark purple. Wild dark-yellow grasses lined the muddy bank. To anyone who had spent more than a little time in the Queen's lands, it was the most beautiful sight imaginable.

Further upstream the river split in two and re-joined further on. The island in the middle was the village of Curlkiss. Once it had been a proud and prosperous town, if small. Now it was dishevelled and falling apart. There were still many Fairies living in the town, kind souls who remembered the days of contentment under the old Queen.

In those days, there was no stigma about how people looked. In every species in every world, whether Goblin, Fairy, Elf, Boggart, Gnome, Brownie, Cat or even Human, there are those who are different. Sometimes a person is born, unable to see, hear, walk, or in the case of Fairies, to fly. Sometimes people have accidents and can lose arms or legs or wings.

On Fayre, the word Pixie used to mean 'strong legs.' It was a kind term for those who were born without wings or had lost them in an accident.

But the new Queen made the word an insult and changed it to mean anyone she didn't like and to treat them like slaves. The Fairies of Curlkiss still treated the Pixies as equals and helped them when they could.

In no time at all Mai was heading south with Joi, who promised to go to the outcast village, but no further. Tai and Chai found many in Curlkiss who were fit and willing to help. So they prepared to set off cross-country and join up with Bailey. Though not knowing exactly where Bailey would be, worried them.

***

As Mai journeyed south, the Boggarts were approaching the castle. The street was wide and bright. The great flagstones, which made up the road, seemed to be made of gold, at least from a distance. Seen close up, it was just cheap gold paint that was flaking away showing what had once been beautiful creamy white and strawberry-red stones.

On either side of the avenue was a low stone wall, crudely painted in the same cheap pink as the castle and beyond this was more of the astroturf and a line of

The road to the City/Castle of Fayre

trees. At first, the Boggarts thought that they must be real, but as they got closer, they noticed they all looked the same.

They were made of fibreglass, another invention of Humans, which they often use nowadays for the outside of cars and aeroplanes. These trees were painted a very convincing brown and on the branches were stuck perfect little green leaves and hanging underneath these were perfectly round plastic fruit.

Being so close to the castle, the traffic both on the road and above it was rapidly increasing. Fairies of all sorts were rushing about above.

On the carriageway, many Pixies were sadly pushing heavy carts or carrying heavy bundles. Some were even pulling carriages in which wealthy Fairies were sitting. (The Fairies inside must have been both rich and lazy. I mean Fairies can fly, and I know what I would prefer.)

It was getting harder and harder for the Boggarts to hide the Nymph. Quickly and quietly while the road was deserted for a few precious moments, a few of them went to the far side of a tree and made a hole in it. Fibreglass is strong, but there is not much that can stand a kicking from a gang of Boggarts. When the Nymph was safely inside, the Boggarts approached the Castle-city of Fayre. This is what they saw.

The avenue ran right up to and through the castle gates. Before entering the gates, the road had to go over a narrow bank. The bank was just wide enough to allow one cart at a time to pass over. Other than this narrow track, a moat went around the rest of the castle. (Just in case you don't know, a moat is a ditch dug around a castle and filled with water to stop people from getting up to the walls.)

This particular moat had fountains, which were filled with glitter that sparkled in the sun. It was far too wide to jump, and there was nothing but a smooth wall on the other side. This was the castle's outside wall (which is also called a curtain wall). It was very tall and very thick. Many towers were built into it with windows looking in all directions. Looking at the stonework, the Boggarts could see no cracks or ledges or handholds, no way for them to climb over.

The main entrance seemed to be the only way in or out. The entrance consisted of an arched gatehouse some 20 meters long. At the far end were huge, pink-painted metal doors. Guards stood beside them, ready to slam them shut in an emergency, although right now they looked half asleep. At the front of the archway, a portcullis could be lowered. (A portcullis is a large iron wall, which can be dropped down in an emergency.)

The Boggarts walked as bold as they could under the portcullis and up to the gates, hoping the guards wouldn't inspect them too carefully. They shouldn't have worried. The guards took hardly any notice of anything at all.

On the other side of the gate, the avenue branched into three roads. One led to the right and seemed to go on and on out of sight. It appeared to the Boggarts that the houses along this road looked poorer, and the further the houses were from the gates, the more dishevelled they got.

Not far from the junction, the paving on this road came to an end, and the carriageway itself became a bare track, which many grim-faced guards were patrolling.

The middle street was full of shops of every kind. The stores nearer the gate were the finest, with hat shops, clothes shops, and posh restaurants.

As the road went on, the shops became more your everyday sort. Down this street, many Fairies went to and fro. They were busy buying the latest fashions and admiring themselves in mirrors. Behind them, poor Pixies carried their boxes and waited on them.

The third road, however, went to the left. It was the shortest of the streets. Here the houses were large and luxurious. There were banks, armouries, treasuries, mansions, and courts. The guards here were wearing the shiniest armour and had the brightest buttons. Here and there were Pixies in rags washing the cobblestones, and the guards were ready with sticks in case any of them stopped working.

At the far end was the castle's keep, which was the Seelie Court of the Fairy Queen herself. This was the place where the throne room could be found and where the Queen would make her judgements. (A keep is like a castle inside a castle.) The keep was square with a tall tower at each corner. Each tower was tall enough to see out over the curtain wall. Right at the back was a fifth tower taller even than the others. The top of this tower had a pointed roof whose tiles shone with gold.

There was only one entrance to the keep, and it was almost as well-guarded as the main gate. Its iron door was much smaller than the one on the main gate, but it was pure metal, cold and hard.

In all the streets, from the poorest to the richest, banners showing the beautiful and noble face of the Queen flew and it seemed she was smiling sweetly at everyone and everything. In a way she was. Everywhere they had looked, there were guards beyond count.

Quietly, the smallest of the Boggarts snuck out to give the news to the Nymph, while the rest quietly mingled with the crowds and waited.

***

The Sprites fought against the current. The further they went, the faster it got. And they started to fear they would get swept away.

Exhausted, they struggled up a side pipe and came out in a shallow pool just like the one they had left. As they looked around, they noticed the bright pink walls of the castle seemed to surround them. A small giggle made them jump. A Fairy child had spotted them while gazing into the water.

"Look, mama," the child cried. "There are Fairies made of water in the pool."

The Sprites ducked out of sight just in time, The Fairy's mother came over, looking down its nose.

"Don't be silly," said the older Fairy in an angry hush. "If the guards hear you making up stories, you'll be turned into a Pixie."

"But Mama, I'm not lying," the child cried as its mother dragged it away. As soon as the coast was clear, the Sprites disappeared back down the pipe.

***

When the Nymph reported to Bailey, the news was disheartening, and he considered calling the whole thing off. It was while he was trying to work out what to do next, that a Fairy arrived. It flew into the middle of Bailey's group. No sooner had it landed than Goblins and Guardians surrounded it.

"Where is Bailey?" the Fairy asked. "I have a message for him from Tai."

"I am Bailey, and who are you?"

"My name is Kai," the young Fairy said as she bowed low to Bailey. "My father is the Mayor of a small town called Curlkiss. Tai is there. She is heading towards the city with some of our townsfolk: thirty pixies and twenty fairies at least. They are trying to time it, so they meet you on the road near the castle. But you must leave in the next few minutes.

"Fifty will help a lot," said Bailey, "but I admit I hoped for more."

"And you may well get it," the little Fairy replied. "Your friend Mai has journeyed on to the outcast village. They say there are hundreds of Pixies there. Nobody knows how many to be sure, but they all hate the Queen."

It was an awkward moment for Bailey. He knew in his heart that they wouldn't get another chance to rescue Shadow, but at the same time, he didn't want to see anyone get hurt. After a moment's thought, he gave orders to the Nymph who rushed away and then turned to the rest of the group and explained what he had learnt. Their faces dropped as the enormity of the task ahead was made clear to them, though they brightened a little to hear that help was on its way.

"I know to some of you it may seem foolish," Bailey said, "but we must try and rescue Shadow. We must try and save the Pixies. We must try to put an end to this pointless hatred, and we won't get another chance."

The army moved off, all but the remaining Water Sprite, who returned to Kapul-Tok to let them know Bailey's decision and to warn them that the army might not be coming back.

Chapter 11
Rise of the Guardians

Bailey and the army walked onwards. Now and then they would pass a Pixie, busy with some chore, who would join them. Not far from the castle, they saw the group coming from Curlkiss.

It was with over 300 behind him that Bailey reached the city. The guards, of course, had seen them from afar. Bailey and the others ran as fast as they could, but the portcullis was lowered, and the metal doors shut with a clang just as they arrived. Bailey's army was at the gates, but there was no way inside.

'*Now they know we are here,*' thought Bailey, 'what will their next move be?' Behind him, over three hundred Gnomes, Brownies, Pixies Fairies and Guardians wondered the same thing.

Silence hung in the air like a cloud. Bailey's army was getting impatient, they had worked themselves up for a battle, and now there was nothing but high pink silent walls looming over them.

Eventually, a small shape appeared on the battlements above the gate.

"In the name of the Queen," the little voice cried down to them. "We burble... mumble, mumble."

"Speak up!" shouted one of the Pixies. "We can't hear a blooming thing."

The Fairy seemed to turn round to talk to someone, and when it turned back, it had a large silver funnel held close to its mouth.

"IN THE NAME OF THE QUEEN," the Fairy's voice boomed. "Why have you come in force as enemies into our land?"

Bailey sat waiting for someone else to answer before remembering it was up to him.

"We... CAN YOU HEAR ME UP THERE?" Bailey shouted.

"YES," called back the Fairy spokesperson. "LOUD AND CLEAR."

"Firstly, we have come, to bring back the Guardian called Shadow, who you have abducted from our world illegally," said Bailey.

"Well..." began the Fairy, but Bailey interrupted him.

"Secondly, there is the matter of the war between Goblins and Elves. It has come to light that your administration instigated it."

"We never," said the Fairy, but before it could say any more Bailey spoke again.

"Then there is the persecution and ill-treatment of your brothers and sisters whom you cast out and call Pixies."

"That is no concern of yours!" snapped the Fairy.

"Lastly," said Bailey, "there are your attempts to make all worlds like this one, which we consider an act of war. Even now, my world is becoming full of fakery. Fake flowers and fake food, fake people, and fake lives. You are to blame!"

With that, the Fairy laughed.

"Your world?" It said with a sneer, "You mean the Human's World. It has not been hard to whisper in their ears while they sleep and make them dream of the same things we do."

"It ends now," said Bailey.

There was an uncomfortable silence. Then the Fairy laughed long and hard.

"It will indeed end this very day," it said, "We have cells enough for all of you in our dungeons. None of you will ever return to your home-worlds. Then there will be nothing to stop us."

The Fairy raised its hand in signal and as it waved hundreds upon hundreds of Fairies flew out of every window and every tower.

***

Bailey and the Guardians fought hard, jumping into the air and swiping Fairies around the head. But Bailey had given strict orders that they were to use the minimum force necessary. The Goblins were untouchable, with their shields they made walls and roofs that no Fairy could penetrate; but this meant they could not fight either. The Pixies could not fly, but still had Fairy strength and gave as good as they could, and the few Fairies from Curlkiss were wrestling with guards in the sky; tying their wings together and making them fall to the ground. Fairies are very light, and it hurt them not at all.

***

Near the hollow of the tree, meanwhile, the Gnomes and Brownies were digging. They ripped up the fake rubber grass, trying desperately to reach real soil.

***

The Sprites reached the end of their journey. The pipes had come out into a large open-topped tank. From here another pipe took the water to a pumping room where huge machines pumped the water back to all the fountains.

***

Behind the curtain wall, the Boggarts waited. When it seemed all but a few soldiers were left. The Boggarts turned back to their natural selves. In a whirl of muscles, kilts, and staffs, they had knocked out the remaining gate guards and were making short work of raising the portcullis.

A sudden cry went up as the poor Pixies of the city, angry from their years of torment, pushed open the gates.

"NOW!" shouted Bailey. The army rushed forward. The Goblins had to break ranks; as they ran, a few were picked up and carried away by scores of Fairies.

Almost 250 were still with him, as Bailey made it under the portcullis.

The Fairies had not been idle. As soon as the gates were open, many had flown back and fought with the Boggarts. The Boggarts had fought bravely, but there were too few of them. They were quickly overcome and carried away to the keep and its dungeons. With a crash, the portcullis came down behind Bailey, and before him, the doors shut. They were trapped.

The Fairy who had spoken to them earlier came to the other side of the portcullis and laughed a cruel laugh.

"You will all surrender immediately and then… Wait, what's that voice in my head?"

***

The Gnomes had dug down until they found the real earth. It had been dead now for many years, and it made the Brownies cry to feel how barren and empty the soil felt. As their tears sank into the earth, the Gnomes' root-like toes burrowed into the ground. Old seeds and roots awoke, and suddenly creepers, vines and stalks came slowly sprouting from the barren earth.

"Water!" the Gnomes cried out. "We need water!"

The Nymph heard their cry and shouted out as loud as it could. Everyone for miles around could hear its voice in their minds. The Fairies, the Goblins, the Pixies, the Guardians and of course the Water Sprites.

***

The Sprites knew what to do. In a moment they had jammed the pumping machinery, and suddenly the whole pump room exploded.

Thousands of gallons of water shot up into the sky and began to fall like soft rain. The Gnomes and Brownies ripped up even more of the rubber grass as the rain fell.

Even as the Fairy Captain looked up in awe of the sudden rain, huge vines and creepers came ripping through the ground all around the castle. They grew right up to the gate. Burrowed into the stonework and in no time at all, the gatehouse, portcullis, and gates lay in ruins. Bailey's army streamed into the city.

The rain stopped as suddenly as it had started. Many of the Fairies had been caught up in the deluge and retreated on foot to dry their wings.

Bailey pressed his advantage while it lasted and with many more Pixies and even a few of the poorer Fairies flocking behind him they fought street by street.

***

The night had come, and the bright moons of Fayre shone down, but Bailey didn't notice. His only thought was of getting to the keep and finding Shadow.

Slowly but surely, he pushed the Fairies back. Many Goblins and Pixies, and even a few Guardians, had been carried off to the dungeons. Bailey was relieved to see Mai arrive with all of the outcast Pixies (and a good few friendly Fairies). They were tired from a hard run to the city, but less tired than many and ready to fight.

***

The sky was brightening, and dawn was not far off as they finally approached the keep, but Bailey's heart sank. Where his forces were tired and sore, there were yet hundreds of fresh Fairy warriors.

Then a sudden cry split the night and the skies were filled with dark shapes, shapes with red eyes. The sound of mighty wings beating air filled their ears and for a moment, Bailey didn't know what to make of this new danger. Then with the rising of the sun, the figures on the back of the mighty beasts, whom Bailey hadn't even noticed, blazed into bright light. Bailey, close to panic, was about to order a retreat, but at that moment…

'I'm here brother,' said a familiar voice in Bailey's mind. *'Let us finish this.'* With a mighty growl, Bailey leapt back into the battle.

***

You would almost have mistaken them for dragons, but they were bats. Giant bats from the mountains of Alfhiem fell screeching and squeaking in amongst the flying and fleeing Fairies. On the back of each was a shining Elf holding the reins with one hand and a mighty staff in the other. Upon one, Gothrick sat with Scruff before him. (Scruff had left Ghaz'on in Kapul-Tok with a very relieved Dzukaluke.)

Many of the guards, seeing the way their fortunes were fairing, gave up. Some, who had never really liked being a guard anyway, turned and helped Bailey, tearing off their armour. Eventually, the combined armies of the Elves and Goblins, Guardians and Pixies (not to mention the many friendly Fairies) beat back the last resistance. On the steps of the keep, the last of the Grand Army of Fayre surrendered.

***

Scruff and Bailey rushed to each other and nuzzled. Then, noticing all the faces smiling at them, they turned back to the business at hand.

Bailey called for the Gnomes, Brownies, and Water Sprites to come to the keep so all could play a part' but Scruff asked him to wait for a few minutes.

Shortly after, a cloud appeared on the horizon, and as it got bigger, Bailey could see it was another group of bats. Each carried one of the Elders who had come through from Kapul-Tok, in Scruff's wake. There was WhooWhee of the Brownies, The Chairman of the Guardians, Burgh, and several others of the Goblin council. The Chief Maiden of the Water Sprites and the King and Queen of the Elves all arrived. (The Chief of the Boggarts had been there all the time, and Gnomes have no leader as they work as one.)

Bailey had expected one of these great leaders to take over. Instead, they all bowed to him and Scruff and stood quietly, waiting for the kittens.

"Give yourselves up and face fair justice!" cried Bailey at the high pink walls of the keep. There was no answer.

One of the Fairies, a young guard, called Fai who had only ever wanted to be a gardener, offered to open the door from inside and Bailey agreed. She flew off, and a short while later there was a clang as the door opened.

Bailey and Scruff went in, followed by representatives of all the kinds and creatures there. A short passage ended in a hall, from which doors led to all of the towers, rooms, and passageways.

"Does anyone know the way to the dungeons?" asked Bailey.

An old Pixie put up his hand, and Bailey beckoned him to come forward.

"Will you show Tai and me the way?" said Scruff. "We want to release Shadow and the other prisoners." The old Pixie nodded enthusiastically.

"Take some Goblins and Elves with you," said Bailey. "I'm going to find the Queen." Scruff nodded and rushed off. The rest of them went forward.

In the throne room of the Seelie Court, the throne was empty. A few old Fairies in regal robes rushed around hurriedly burning documents. A loud, vicious growl from Bailey and they all stood still.

"Round them up," Bailey said. WhooWhee flexed her many arms, and in no time at all she and the Brownies had them all cowering in the corner. Bailey suspected she was rather enjoying herself.

Behind the throne was a small door leading to a spiral staircase. Bailey beckoned for Mai to come with him, and the pair continued up the stairs until he had reached the tallest chamber of the highest tower.

At the top was a large double door. Two guards outside crossed their staffs to bar the way.

"Really?" asked Bailey, looking up at them. They looked into his eyes, then slowly put down their staffs, and ran away.

Bailey pushed open the door. Inside was what would have been (for a Fairy) a spacious apartment, but like everywhere else the old had been covered up. The walls were all vibrant, unnatural pinks with gold highlights. The room they were now in had two doors leading from it. The entrance to the right led to a bathroom. Inside was a sunken bath, which would have been spacious for even the biggest human. To Mai and Bailey, it was almost a swimming pool. The floor was littered with plastic bottles of shampoos and conditioners and age-reducing creams.

The door on the left was closed. Bailey knocked, and after a few moments, a voice called out, "Enter!"

Bailey and Mai entered cautiously. The room was a bedroom, and the sickly perfume was at its most potent. Bailey had to breathe through his mouth to stop his head from spinning. But he could taste it on his tongue and had to stifle the urge to bring up a furball.

The room had massive windows, which looked out over the fake fields and meadows that surrounded the castle. Of the city itself, only one of the towers of the keep and a small section of curtain wall could be seen.

The bedroom was circular, and to Bailey's, surprise seemed to be covered in pictures of fairies from the human world. There was one Bailey recognised from Kirsty's nightgown; a blonde fairy in a short green dress with white slippers; This same fairy in different poses adorned posters on all the walls.

The bed was empty, on the further side of the room was a dressing table in front of which, a figure sat in a long green dressing gown combing its long blonde hair. What struck Bailey as odd was that all around the dressing table there were strange white heads, all but one had a different colour and length of hairstyle.

Bailey and Mai walked up, expecting to see the Queen of the Fairies, whose face shone from banners on every post in the city. But when they were close enough to see her reflection, Mai let out a gasp.

The face in the mirror looked like a Child's toy; Its skin was waxy, its cheekbones and lips were frozen in a permanent smile and Its eyes were stuck wide, though they still shone with the light of Fairy-kind. Whether the Queen was surprised at the interruption they couldn't tell.

"Beautiful am I not?" The Queen said. Her lips hardly moved as she spoke through her frozen smile. Her eyes never leaving her own reflection. Bailey didn't know what to say.

"Beautiful?" said Mai at length. "Do you really think what you have done to yourself is beautiful?"

The Queen finally looked around, her brow furrowed ever so slightly, and her nose wrinkled.

"What's the meaning of this?" the Queen asked. "Who are you? How dare you enter the royal apartment? Guards! Guards! Come quickly!"

Mai pushed passed Bailey and looked with disgust at the Queen.

"I'm afraid there are no guards left," said Mai. "you're going to have to answer for everything you have done."

The Queen sneered.

"I am Queen," she said. "I am the law."

"Your 'law' is the reason my wings got cut off," said Mai.

"I don't trouble myself with the day-to-day decisions at my court," the Queen replied. "If they cut off your wings, they must have had an excellent reason."

"They said I was not pretty enough," said Mai, "that we represent the Queen's beauty, but look at you."

"Yes, am I not perfect?" said the Queen. "The people love me."

"You *were* beautiful," said Mai. "Nobody outside of your keep has any idea what you have become."

"Rubbish," said the Queen. "They make a portrait of me every few months and hang copies of it all around the city."

"Your majesty," said Mai. "They have been showing the people the same portrait of you for the last hundred years, the one where you DO look radiant and beautiful."

"I have had enough of this," the Queen snapped back, "GUARDS! GUARDS! Where are my GUARDS?"

"Nobody is coming for you, Your Majesty," Bailey growled. "But don't worry, you won't be alone for long," Bailey whispered his plan to Mai, and the little Pixie actually giggled.

***

Far below in the dungeons, Scruff had found Shadow. The cell she was in was too small for a cat, and after being stuck in there for months, she was thin, fragile, stiff, and sore.

Opening the door hadn't taken much. The jail-keeper had refused at first, but Scruff told him she had not eaten all day and licked her lips. He soon changed his mind.

Some Elves and Goblins helped to get Shadow up the stairs. Tired as she was, she demanded to know what trouble Bailey and Scruff had been getting into and tutted as Scruff gave her a hasty account, but her eyes sparkled with pride.

Meanwhile, the Elves and Goblins worked together to free the rest of the prisoners. Tai finally found her friend Nim, looking dishevelled and forlorn but healthy. In no time at all, the prisoners were free.

***

Bailey had gone downstairs to make arrangements, leaving Mai to watch over the Queen who wailed like a spoilt child.

"But things are almost perfect" cried the Queen, stamping her foot. "You mustn't stop me now."

"We have to, it's the only way to save our world." Said Mai "Can't you see that? What is this obsession you have with plastic?"

"Plastic is perfect. Have you seen the wonderful dolls human children carry? They never get old; they never crack or crumble or age. They make playhouses for them out of plastic with gardens that never need mowing which are always neat and tidy. Plastic is the answer to everything."

Mai was about to give the Queen a piece of her mind when Bailey made his presence known.

"I think it's about time your people saw you in the flesh again," he said.

The Queen looked up anxiously as the sound of beating wings came from outside. Giant claws ripped the top of the tower. The Queen leapt upon her bed in fear, the claws gripped the bed, gently lifting the screaming Queen and carrying her down.

There was quite a crowd around the bottom of the tower. The Fairies and Pixies gasped in horror to see what had happened to their Queen. The Queen they saw in magazines, posters, and banners all around the city, was vibrant and glamorous. The creature wearing a crown in front of them now looked little more than a child's doll. Her beautiful hair was shown up as cheap nylon in the morning light. Her wings drooped under the weight of sequins and rhinestones.

Scruff and Bailey came up and stood on either side of the Queen. Bailey was about to say something when he saw Tai in the crowd and beckoned him up. Tai looked at the Queen with disgust in his eyes.

"You see before you a sick Queen," cried out Tai to the crowd. "While she should be pitied for what she has done to herself, she must answer for what she has done to Fayre, for her obsession with beauty. An obsession which has distorted her view until she mutilates Fairies for not reaching her standards and yet cannot see how she has mutilated herself."

"Nonsense," cried the Queen. "I am the very meaning of beauty." The huge talon of an Elven Bat tapped her lightly on the shoulder and the Queen silenced her protest.

"A Queen who cut off my wings, just because I disagreed with her. A Queen who has turned our world into a bad joke of the beautiful place it used to be. I say it ends now, this very day."

The crowd roared, and Bailey stepped forward.

"But it's not my fault," cried the Queen. "It was my advisors - they did it all."

Bailey nodded, and all of her advisors were brought forward.

"Your Majesty," said Scruff. "If you are truly a fit Queen, then you are responsible for the actions of your ministers. If not, then you are not fit to be Queen."

The Queen opened her mouth but, seeing no way out of the trap that Scruff had laid, she slowly closed it again.

"It seems your world, like the human world has become obsessed with plastic." said Bailey, "But how many of you know that plastic is killing the human world."

"I hear my human worry about it every day. It's polluting their oceans, killing their fish. It destroys the countryside. Take these *precious* dolls which your Queen has become obsessed with. Most of these dolls end up on rubbish tips, which grow and grow until there may one day be nothing but rubbish. Right now, some humans are fighting to save their world; whilst others, like your Queen, are so blinded by greed they no longer care for anything but themselves... Would *you* see your world become like that?

The crowd were silent. It was some moments before they could take on board the enormity of what Bailey had said.

"As you have been so willing to take one of the worst things of human society," said Scruff, "today we are going to share one of the best things that humans have invented. It's called democracy."

The crowd looked confused.

"There are two choices open to you," she said. "The first is to go back to the way things were. If you choose that, any who want to come with us will be allowed to, and then the world of Fayre will be cut off from Kapul-Tok, and the Charnwood. Every other world will be lost to you. For none of us would want anything to do with you." At this, there was much grumbling from the crowd.

"The second," said Bailey, "is to choose leaders from amongst yourselves. Create laws to ensure nobody can ever take away your rights. If you choose this, we will help you." The mumbling from the crowd now seemed more hopeful, even optimistic.

"Even better," said Bailey, "if you choose that route, you will be welcome to travel to worlds as you once did when Fairies were loved."

"Some of you may even become Guardians and help protect your world and others," said Scruff. "For though the Cats of Charnwood Forest are the last of the Guardians, we were not the first. There used to be Guardians from every race."

"Even Humans?" shouted a young Pixie.

"I believe there were one or two, Thousands of years ago," said Scruff "But after all, we do have some standards."

The crowd laughed, and here and there the Fairies and Pixies started smiling as they thought of all the opportunities they could have.

"As for the Queen, her advisors and supporters," said Bailey, "you can keep them… or exile them if you wish. We can find them a habitable world and leave them there to do as they please, with no way back. It's your choice."

"We will make these decisions together," said Mai. "Everyone in the land of Fayre will get to vote, old or young, rich or poor, Fairy or Pixie."

Bailey turned to go, but Scruff turned back to the crowd.

"One more thing!" she roared, "No more of this Pixies and Fairies rubbish. You are all one people, with equal rights and responsibilities."

With that, Bailey and Scruff helped a tired and wobbly Shadow onto the back of a mighty Elven Bat, and Gothrick flew her back to the pond.

***

As they passed through Kapul-Tok, Scruff introduced Shadow to Ghaz'on and Dzukaluke. The Goblins insisted that they stay for dinner. Dzukaluke made them an exquisite meal. Shadow insisted on hearing everything in full. She listened intently to Bailey's description of the Land of Fading Memories and the 'Other'.

"I wonder," she said under her breath. "I promised I would never forget you Taliesin, and I never have."

Scruff saw that Ghaz'on was taking lots of notes as they told Shadow their tale and before they left, she asked the young Goblin what it was doing.

"I was thinking, although I still want to be a parent one day, I might also like to be a writer. I've already started on a book about your adventures."

Ghaz'on pulled out a pile of paper. On the first page was written in both Human and Goblin.

'The Cats of Charnwood Forest.'

Scruff smiled and said it sounded like the perfect job for an inquisitive young Goblin, (and if you ever read this again, you will now know who your humble narrator is).

Finally, the three departed, with Bailey and Scruff promising to visit again soon.

***

Half an hour later, Shadow finally stood in her very own garden again.

The Chairman was waiting, and they greeted each other, pressing their foreheads together as cats will often do with their friends. They spoke quietly for a while, after which the Chairman came over to the two kittens.

"Well, Bailey, Scruff, you have performed admirably," he said, nodding to each in turn, "and with more courage than I have seen in many years."

The old cat took a moment to straighten his fur and whiskers, which if anything made him look even wirier.

"It is therefore with great pleasure, that I bestow upon you the rank of full Guardians," he said. "You are kittens no longer. You are Cats of Charnwood Forest." Then after licking them both gently on the forehead, he left.

"Congratulations," said a smiling Shadow. "I'm sure you will do great things in the future."

"With you to guide us, we will," said Scruff.

"Guide you? You who rescued me? You who defeated the Fairy army and brought peace to the worlds? No, I'm afraid you're on your own. I'm retiring.

I'm no longer your teacher, but I will always be your friend."

Tenacious/Mum

With that, Shadow jumped up at Pippa's windowsill and called for her human.

"Where have you been, you silly cat?" cried Pippa, with tears running down her cheeks. "You silly old cat." Shadow jumped inside and was gone.

"Oh well," said Scruff to Bailey. "Just you and me left. Let's go home."

As they climbed through the cat-flap, their noses twitched, something was wrong. Cautiously they crept into the living room. Kirsty and Jon were sitting together on the settee.

"Oh, Bailey, Willow, where have you been?" asked Kirsty. "I have some fantastic news. Jon has moved in, and we are going to get married." Before the cats could even react to this first piece of news, Kirsty continued.

"And he has bought a special someone with him," she said.

From out of the kitchen, a cat appeared. It arched its back when it saw them.

"Who are you?" it hissed, baring its teeth, and trying to look big; Its black and gold fur standing on end,

Though the newcomer was much smaller than Bailey and Scruff remembered, there was no mistaking her. The Cats of Charnwood Forest looked at each other and back to the newcomer.

"Mum?" they said.

The End.

~MAP~

covering those parts of the Charnwood appearing in this book

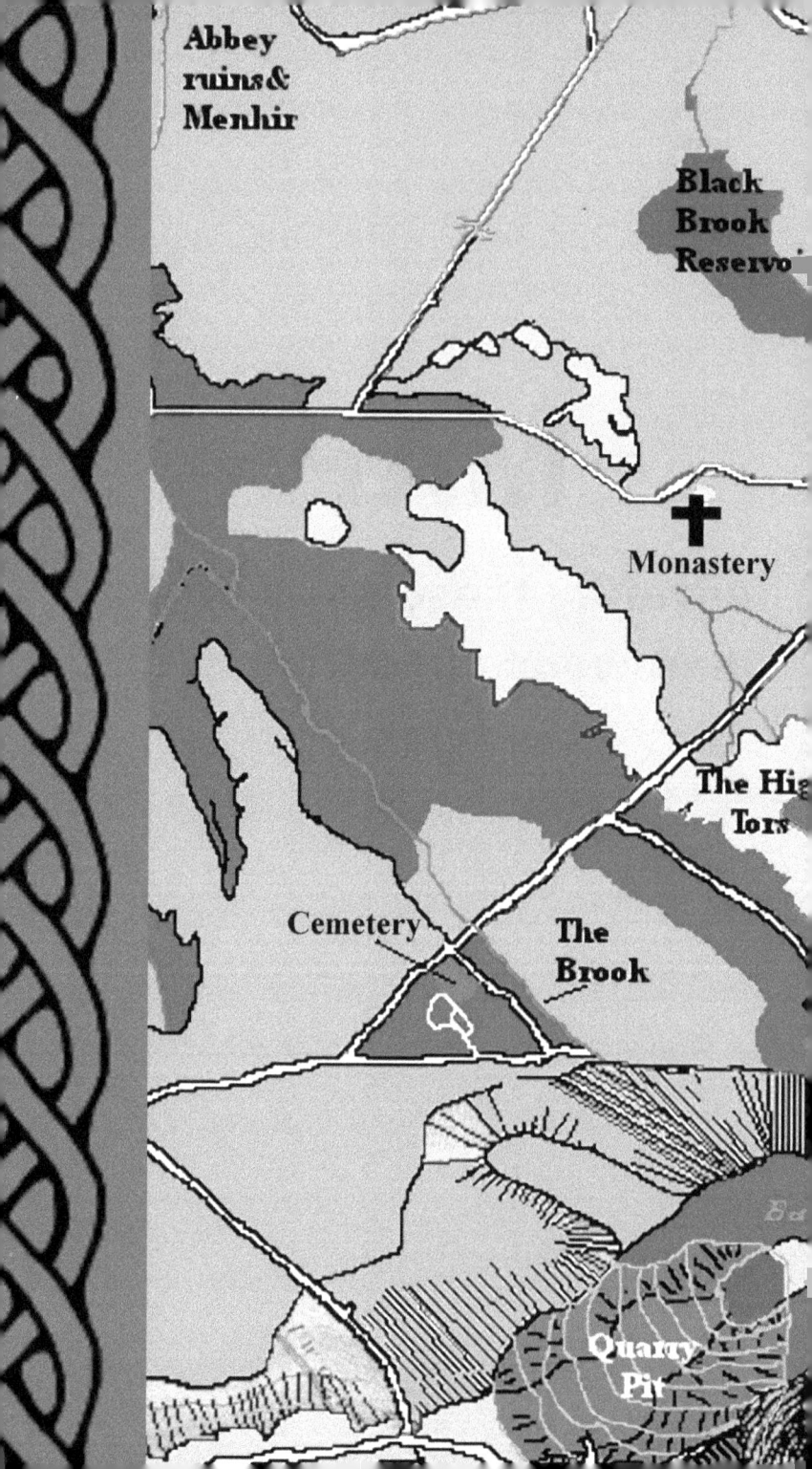

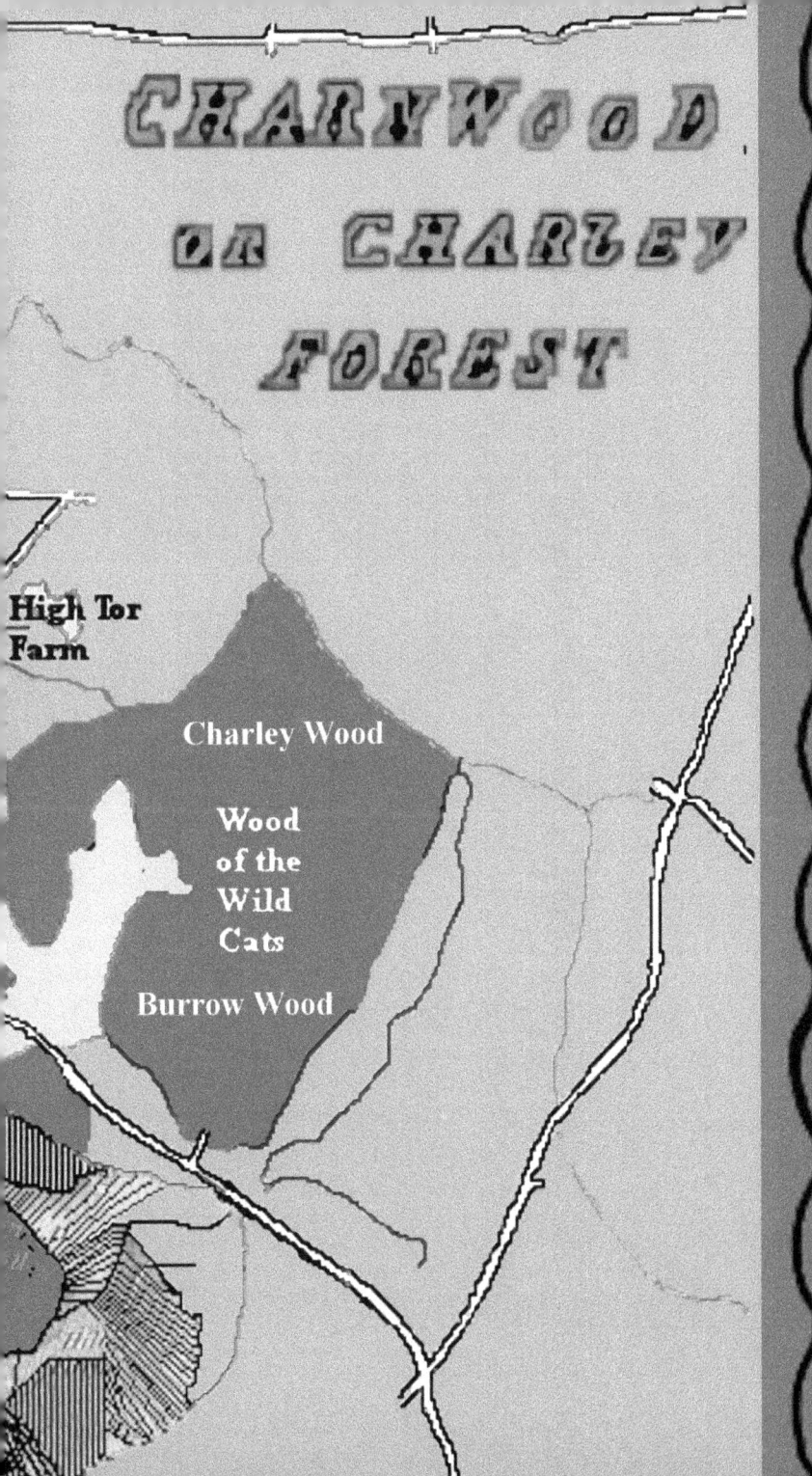

Explore the Further Adventures of Bailey and Scruff in...

Constantine

JÖTUNHEIM

The Cats of Charnwood Forest Book 2

www.ingramcontent.com/pod-product-compliance
Lightning Source LLC
Chambersburg PA
CBHW041139110526
44590CB00027B/4069